BURY MY BONES BUT KEEP MY WORDS

BURY MY BONES
BUT KEEP MY WORDS

African Tales for Retelling

Retold by Tony Fairman
Illustrated by Meshack Asare

"Bury my bones but keep my words"
(Luo proverb: Kenya)

Henry Holt and Company ● New York

Text copyright © 1991 by Tony Fairman
Illustrations copyright © 1991 by Meshack Asare
Map illustration copyright © 1991 by Claire Jones

First published in the United States in 1992 by Henry Holt and Company, Inc.,
115 West 18th Street, New York, New York 10011.
Published simultaneously in Canada by Fitzhenry & Whiteside Ltd.,
91 Granton Drive, Richmond Hill, Ontario L4B 2N5.
Originally published in Great Britain by HarperCollins Publishers, Limited.
Published by arrangement with HarperCollins Publishers, Limited.

Library of Congress Cataloging-in-Publication Data
Fairman, Tony.
Bury my bones but keep my words: African tales for retelling /
retold by Tony Fairman; illustrated by Meshack Asare.
Includes bibliographical references.
Summary: A collection of traditional African tales, including
"The Man with a Tree on His Head," "There's One Day for the Victim,"
and "The Two Swindlers."
ISBN 0-8050-2333-X
1. Tales—Africa. [1. Folklore—Africa.] I. Asare, Meshack,
1945– ill. II. Title.   PZ8.1.F18Bu 1992   398.2′096—dc20   92-25014

Printed in the United States of America
on acid-free paper. ∞

First American edition

1 3 5 7 9 10 8 6 4 2

CONTENTS

Contents

I'd like to thank Donald Lowle for the hieroglyphs, and Mick and Sue Nixon for help with the music on page 191, and my sister, Jenny Fairman, for help with everything.

A note about storytelling: If you intend to retell these tales, or if (May the bones of our storytelling ancestors rest in peace!) you should actually read them aloud as tales, ignore the boxes. They contain information and atmosphere, and are not part of the tales. To develop their pupils' oral ability, teachers can try the following methods: 1) Tell one tale to one group and another tale to another group. Let each group revise among themselves the tale they have just heard, then pair each child with a child from the other group. 2) Divide the tale into two or three parts and tell each part to a different group. Then let them reconstruct the tale. The references to African life and circumstances are as accurate in spirit and detail as I can make them and are intended to give impressions of daily life in various parts of Africa.

This book is for Mrs Truphosa Ambogo Namusei,
who began it all by telling me two of these tales, and
for all my friends and students in Africa.

AFRICA

The Gambia

Egypt

RIVER NILE

Nigeria

Kenya

Nambia

Botswana

SOUTH AFRICA

Scale

0   1000   2000 km

0   500   1000 miles

Erm! Your attention please!

If I can just get a word in before the story-tellers carry you off... My name's Tony, by the way. I'm the writer, and I think I'd better print the rest of this word-in-your-ear.

I really ought not to be writing these tales down; I ought to be telling them because these are African tales and in Africa people usually don't write tales like these down, or read them: they tell them. When these tales are told they come alive; they sing, they dance, they laugh, they move, they rattle along. I know; I've told some of these tales myself to children in England and we sing, we move, we laugh and the tales rattle along. But a tale in a book is like a drum in a museum; it's silent, it's dead, it's just there doing nothing. And that's sad because tales are for telling; they're for laughter, they're for singing, for sharing.

So, after you've read these tales, I want you to take them off the page and give them life. Go and tell them, share them – and all the other tales you know – with your friends and anybody who will listen. Telling is more fun than reading because each telling is different. You can never tell a tale in the same way to different listeners.

To make it easier for you and show you how it's done, I've tried to describe people and places in Africa where the tales are being told. I've described night time

11

in Africa, the houses, the parents and children, the weather, the sights, sounds and smells you would notice if you were there, listening to the tales. I've written songs you can sing, just as Africans sing, with a chorus and a lead singer. And I've shown how the listeners behave during the tale: how they sing, move and ask questions. Everybody joins in, helping the tale to come out. And that's how tales are told in Africa.

Away you go now!

Hang on! Hang on! Come back a minute! Just another tiny word-in-your-ear.

In these tales, you're going to meet a lot of strange-looking African names. But don't be scared of them; they're quite easy to read really, because African spelling is very simple, much simpler than English spelling. All you have to remember is to say each letter in the same way each time you see it.

For example, whenever you see the letters *a:e:i:o:u:* you must always pronounce them with the same sound: *a* is like "cat", *e* is like "let", *i* is like "piece" or "see", *o* is like "hot" and *u* is like "moo".

Milembé = mee-lem-beh	*Modisé* = Mod-dee-seh
Awiti = A-wee-tee	*Hodi* = Hod-dee
Aleikum = A-lay-koom	*Linani* = Lee-nan-nee
	Nyar-upoko = Near-oo-pock-co
	Dubulihasa = Doo-boo-lee-hass-sa
	Kabiyesi = Cab-bee-yes-see
	Musiguku = Moo-see-goo-koo

Easy, isn't it?

Now try this long one: Ran-kwee-deeng-wan-neh. *Rankwi-dingwane. Rankwi-dingwane.*

There you go!

12

· 1 ·

Nyar-upoko

Shall we go to Africa . . . ? . . .
Shall we . . . ? . . .
Well then, imagine night. You can shut your eyes if
you like. A warm night. Don't be afraid, it isn't dark.
Imagine a moon, a full round silver-yellow moon up
there shining down on us.

It's not so dark now. Sort of greyish; silver greys,
light greys and dark greys. You can make out grey
shapes, the shapes of bushes and trees – tall dark
feathery eucalyptus trees, rustling in the light breeze.
The breeze is warm and brings the sweet scent of night
flowers – frangipani.

A small shadow moves – a dog, two dogs. No, one
dog and its shadow upside-down. Wherever the shadow
goes, the dog goes too. The dog sniffs its shadow and
the shadow sniffs its dog. Their noses touch for a
moment. Pfff! The dog and its shadow move on.

Keep going. We're not quite there yet. This is night
in Africa – a full moon night, the time in Africa for
telling stories outside.

Now imagine noise – the night in Africa is never
silent – lots of noise, noise all round. Millions and
millions of insects: busy *dudus*, chizzing and deedling

13

all night long. Some little and others not so little, all night long they never stop telling stories, the noisy *dudus*. And frogs too, always warking. Sometimes a *dudu* chizzes so loud and near your eardrum humzzz.

We're almost there now. Do you still want to go there . . . ? . . .

Well, now imagine two children, a girl and a boy, and their grandma, coming out of the house. "Here children, come and sit by me," says Grandma. "I'll tell you about Nyar-upoko, the love child. Sit here my children, and listen."

Here we are at last, sitting under the silver-yellow moon, and all round us the everlasting *dudus*.

Grandma sits down slowly on the story stool on the sunset side of the house. "Ooof! That's good," she says. "How this warm wall oils my old bones."

Her grandchildren, Awiti and Kech, sit cross-legged on the ground next to her. Awiti is two years older than her brother Kech. She is eleven and is in Standard Four at Kamuga Primary School. Kech is in Standard Two and is nine years old.

The silver-grey dog ambles round the compound in the moonshine. It stops to scratch under its armpit and starts hunting a flea.

"Yes, my children," continues Grandma. "Nyar-upoko, the girl who lived by tender loving care. But when people hated her, she grew cold and lifeless and floppy like a dead bird . . . Now my child, run off and bring me a stick from the fire to light my pipe with. We old women like our pipes in the evening."

So Kech runs off into the darkness and comes back with a glowing stick. Grandma lights her long pipe and

14

takes a few puffs. The smoke shines in the moonlight like wavy, silver threads and vanishes.

"And now listen to the story of Nyar-upoko. She was one of ten girls in the same village – growing up together. She wasn't really more beautiful than her nine friends. But she was Love's child, you see. Some people are born like that – full of lovely thoughts and feelings, and they never think evil of themselves or others. It was these lovely thoughts people saw when they looked at Nyar-upoko's face, or when they felt the touch of her hand on their skin.

Well then, when they became old enough, these girls decided to visit the nearest villages to find themselves husbands.

> "Girls don't do that these days,"
> says Awiti.
> "No, they don't and they didn't
> when I was young either," says
> Grandma. "But they did when
> Nyar-upoko was alive. Customs
> and people change. Maybe your
> daughters will do it. Who knows
> what will happen?"

So the girls spent a whole day plaiting each other's hair. Ten different designs they plaited. Some were round like the circles in the water when you throw a stone. Some were whirls and spirals like the coiling fingers of the beanstalk. Some were stars and some were ruler lines like the lines you draw in your school books.

And when the girls had finished, I tell you, my children, their beauty brings tears to my eyes when I think of it. Even queens in paradise don't look like those ten girls did.

The next day the girls washed their bodies and oiled their skins smooth and satin black. They wrapped themselves in lengths of swirling colour which rippled and flickered over their black shoulders. Finally, the ten girls put on their bracelets, beads and bells. Some were made of warm glowing copper; others were rainbow twists of beads. People don't dress like that these days, except for the tourists, and then they only do it for the money. But these ten girls had dressed to find husbands.

They were ready, clinking and jingling in excitement. They set off, single file, Nyar-upoko last, along the path to the nearest village. The eyes of their parents were on them; eyes here, grieving and joyous; eyes there, crying and laughing. Their mothers shrilling:

'Yiri-yiri-yiri-yiiii. Yiri-yiri-yiri-yiiii.'
and singing:

> 'Just look where our daughters are going,
> > (*Chorus*) *Bring back.*
> So lovely like birds on the wing.
> > *Bring back.*
> Our hearts are both grieving and joyous.
> > *Bring back.*
> Oh bring back our daughters to us.
> > *Bring back, bring back,*
> > *O bring back our daughters to us.'*

> Try singing this to the tune of My
> Bonnie Lies Over the Ocean.

And some people cried a little.

"Why did they cry, Grandma?"
asks Kech.
"Well, child," answers Grandma,
"they weren't really crying, not
like you do when you hurt yourself.
Tears also come when people are
very, very happy."

17

And so the girls set off, a line of colours in the grass.
The bells on their ankles were clinking and jingling as
they walked. And they were talking and giggling like
weaver birds.

And when they reached the first village, all the
young men – and many not so young ones — came like
thirsty cattle to water: 'Oo!' they exclaimed. 'Ooo!
Ooooo!' as they gazed and gazed.

Then they remembered their manners: '*Nadi*, girls.
What are your names? The one at the back – let's start
with her.'

Instantly, the other nine girls were jealous. The
colours faded. Their faces grew dark just as the earth
grows dark before a storm. And off they stalked,
straight out of the village. Nyar-upoko followed. She
couldn't stay all by herself in a strange village, could
she?

Outside the village, deep in the bush the nine girls
stopped and crowded round Nyar-upoko, dark, frown-
ing, pouting with hate.

'You! Poko! You're causing us a lot of trouble, you
and your beauty.'

'Poko, you're not a bit more beautiful than us.'

Nyar-upoko stood there, head down as they shouted
at her from all sides.

'No, you're ugly.'

'You're letting us down, Poko.'

And Nyar-upoko fading, getting limper, sagging.

'We'll show you, Poko.'

'We'll turn you into a – a – a

PIPE.'

Their dark anger, their spiteful jealousy came over Nyar-upoko like a cloud of hopelessness. She faded – faded – vanished.

And there on the ground lay a pipe; a dirty, old, black pipe with a long stem carved with a line of lovely gazelles, ga-leaping, ga-leaping, ga-leaping along.

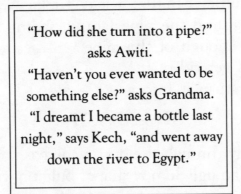

"How did she turn into a pipe?"
asks Awiti.
"Haven't you ever wanted to be something else?" asks Grandma.
"I dreamt I became a bottle last night," says Kech, "and went away down the river to Egypt."

And the leading girl picked up the pipe and stuck it in her belt. Then the nine girls walked on to the next village, their bangles jingling and clinking. And because they were happy once more, the colours returned.

In the second village the same thing happened again. All the young men – and many not so young ones – came like thirsty cattle to water: 'Oo!' they exclaimed, 'Ooo! Ooooo!' as they gazed and gazed.

Then they remembered their manners: '*Nadi*, girls. What are your names? But first, that pipe. That magnificent pipe. Who made it?'

Instantly, the nine girls were jealous. The colours faded. Their faces grew dark just as the earth grows dark before a storm. And off they stalked straight out of the village in a huff as high as a hill.

Out in the bush the leading girl snatched the pipe from her belt. She flung it on the ground and all the girls started kicking dust over it.

'This pipe's causing us a lot of trouble.'

'Those young men don't like girls.'

'If it's pipes they want, they're welcome to it.'

Kick. Shuffle. Shuffle. Kick. Kick. And the dust rising, rising; and the pipe fading, fading.

'I've had enough of this pipe.'

'Yes, let's get rid of it.'

'Yes, let's turn it into a – a – a

CALABASH'

And slowly through the dust a calabash appeared on the ground, an ugly lumpy shape, bulging with carbuncles. But it was decorated with the same beautiful pattern that had been on Nyar-upoko's head.

The nine girls brushed the dust off themselves and then set off in a line to the next village, jingling and clinking as they went. And because they were happy once more, the colours returned. The middle girl carried on her head the lumpy calabash with its lovely pattern.

In the third village all the young men – and many not so young ones – came like thirsty cattle to water: 'Oo!' they exclaimed, 'Ooo! Ooooo!' as they gazed and gazed. Then they remembered their manners: '*Nadi*, girls. What are your names? But first, that beautiful calabash. Who painted the design?'

Hmph! Well, if the nine girls were jealous before, now they were boiling jealous. Their faces grew fat with hatred and the colours died. Off they stumped straight out of the village, barging through the chickens and young men.

Out in the bush they stopped. The middle girl threw the calabash down on the ground and all the girls started kicking dust over it.

'This calabash is causing us a lot of trouble.'

'Whoever heard of young men liking calabashes?'

'Good thing we didn't marry them.'

Kick. Kick. Shuffle. Shuffle. And the dust rising and the calabash fading.

'Smash it. Break it up. Smash! Smash! Smash!'

And they stamped and stamped, stamped, trampled it to pieces.

'Get rid of it. Turn it into a – a – a

DOG.'

And as the dust settled, slowly a dog appeared there on the ground. But what a dog! A mangy thing with eyes floating in green pus. Its tail hung down like sodden string. It was covered with sores and scabs, and under its skin its ribs stuck out like railway lines. Ugh! It makes me shudder to talk of it.

> Grandma puffs at her pipe. Suddenly there's a growl in the darkness behind their backs and the children jump with fright.
> "Shoo! Go away and sleep," says Grandma, waving her pipe at their dog and its shadow. "It's not you we're talking about."

Anyway, there it was, that – that creature of their hatred, the dog. The nine girls brushed themselves down and set off for the next village. And the dog? Well, the dog was so weak that it was stumbling and staggering at every step and was left further and further behind.

In the fourth village things went better for the nine girls. The young men came running like cattle. Then they remembered their manners: '*Nadi*, girls. What are your names?'

And the nine girls introduced themselves and soon found nine young men who were eager to marry them. The young men's mothers also liked the girls and took them back to their homes to arrange the wedding ceremonies.

In all this excitement nobody noticed the dog stagger in late. It collapsed on the ground in a heap of bones and scabby skin, breathing heavily.

But there was a tenth mother whose son hadn't been there when the girls arrived. He'd been out hunting. The mother arrived too late to choose a wife for her son. She was very upset: 'Oh dear, oh dear! Whatever shall I do? My son'll kill me if I don't get him a wife.'

She looked around and noticed the scabby dog and thought to herself: 'Ah well, I suppose I'll have to take that thing. Feed it up and it'll keep the chickens out of the kitchen. Here, boy! Here, boy! Come along with me.' And the dog heaved itself up and staggered after her.

At home, her son came dashing in from his hunting expedition: 'Well, Mother, where's the wife you've brought me?'

His mother just pointed to the skinny dog lying in a corner of the yard.

'What! Is that all you've brought?'

His mother nodded.

'Oh, Mother, why didn't you bring me a wife like all the other mothers did for their sons?' And he kicked the dog savagely. The poor dog was too weak even to whimper.

The next morning the family went out to work in the fields and look after their cattle. Only a little girl was left behind. As the girl was sitting all by herself in the yard, the dog stood up on its hind legs and peeled its skin back slowly, from nose to tail, revealing a beautiful young woman, Nyar-upoko. Nyar-upoko took some corn from a basket and started pounding for the family, cooking for the family. And as she worked she sang:

> 'I am Nyar-upoko,
> a-pounding for the folk-o.
> I am Nyar-upoko,
> a-cooking for the folk-o.
> Calabash. Calabash.
> I love them.'

You can sing this to the tune of Ring-a-ring of roses.

When Nyar-upoko had finished cooking, she sat down with the little girl and they ate the meal, talking together all the time. Then Nyar-upoko washed all the pots and plates, put them on the rack outside the house

to dry in the sun, slipped into the filthy dog skin again and curled up in its corner.

That evening, when her mother came back, the little girl said, 'That dog you found, Mother: there's a beautiful girl who lives in it.'

'Now don't go telling stories, child,' answered her mother. 'You've been sleeping again, haven't you?'

'But it's true. It's true. Her name's Nyar-upoko, and she cooked us a meal and we ate it together and she washed up and then she entered the skin again.'

Well, the little girl's brother wanted a wife too, like the other nine young men in the village. So he decided to stay behind the next day and watch the dog.

The next morning he left the house with the rest of his family. But on tip-toe he returned and quietly, quietly hid in a bush near the gate. Soon he saw the filthy skin peeling slowly off the dog, and out came the most beautiful woman he'd ever seen. And she began to work. She fetched some water and some firewood. She pounded some corn and cooked some porridge, and all the time she worked she sang:

> 'I am Nyar-upoko,
> a-pounding for the folk-o.
> I am Nyar-upoko,
> a-cooking for the folk-o.
> Calabash. Calabash.
> I love them.'

Then Nyar-upoko sat down with the little girl and they ate the meal, talking all the time. After the meal, Nyar-upoko washed all the pots and plates and put them on the rack outside the house to dry, leaving a bit of porridge for the little girl's mother.

And all this time the young man was watching Nyar-upoko from his hiding place. He saw how well she worked, how happy she was, how beautiful she was. And he saw too that she was full of kind thoughts and feelings. As Nyar-upoko was slipping back into the dog skin, the young man ran quickly through the gate. He touched her gently on the arm and said, 'Nyar-upoko, Nyar-upoko.'

Nyar-upoko was frightened and shrank more quickly into the skin. But the young man snatched the skin from her and flung it in the fire. Then he put his arms round her and said, 'Nyar-upoko, stay and be my wife.'

So she stayed.

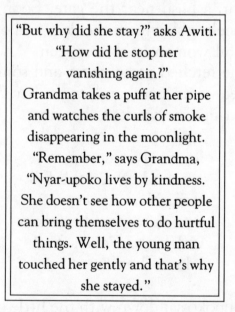

"But why did she stay?" asks Awiti. "How did he stop her vanishing again?" Grandma takes a puff at her pipe and watches the curls of smoke disappearing in the moonlight. "Remember," says Grandma, "Nyar-upoko lives by kindness. She doesn't see how other people can bring themselves to do hurtful things. Well, the young man touched her gently and that's why she stayed."

Well then, when the other nine young men saw how kind and gentle Nyar-upoko was, they each complained of their girls to their mothers: 'Why did you choose this gloomy, grumbling girl for me? Why didn't you take the dog?'

The nine girls heard this and they became gloomier and grumblier than ever. They pouted with jealousy; they puffed with anger. They decided to get rid of Nyar-upoko. 'This time,' they said, 'we won't turn her into anything. We'll kill her.'

So, the next time they went out to fetch firewood from the forest, they asked Nyar-upoko to come with them and she agreed.

On the way to the forest they passed a swamp of papyrus plants. The nine girls stopped and grabbed Nyar-upoko, screaming and yelling in a mad frenzy at the tops of their voices:

> 'By the arms – grab her, grab her.
> (Chorus) Kill. Kill. Kill.
> By the legs – grab her, grab her.
> Kill. Kill. Kill.
> In the swamp – dump her, dump her.
> Kill. Kill. Kill.
> Under water – stamp her, stamp her.
> Kill. Kill. Kill.
> In the mud – tramp her, tramp her.
> Kill. Kill. Kill.'

When there was nothing of Nyar-upoko to see, the girls stopped and cleaned themselves of the dirty water. Then they went on their way to the forest.

Silence. Dead silence.

The swamp was still, not even a bubble popped. The

beautiful papyrus plants slowly drifted back and hid the place where the girls had been stamping.

Silence.

But there was one noise; faint and high, high in the sky. Singing, singing, hovering so high in the sky you couldn't see, only hear. Singing, singing in the sky, hovering was a bird: Ulando, the lark. She had seen everything.

Ulando flew straight to the village. Low over the village square, wings flimmering she hovered, singing, singing:

> 'Someone's drowning,
>   (*Chorus*) *Someone's drowning,*
> In the swamp,
>   *In the swamp,*
> Come and bring your fish nets,
>   *Come and bring your fish nets.*
> Rescue her,
>   *Rescue her.'*

You can sing this to the tune of Frère Jacques.

The young men heard Ulando. They fetched their nets and their rods. Ulando flew off back to the swamp and the young men followed. The lark perched on a papyrus plant near where Nyar-upoko was buried.

The young men put their nets into the water and tried to pull Nyar-upoko out. They tried and tried. But the nets were too weak; they were for catching fish, not young girls. The muck and papyrus clumps were far too heavy.

28

Nyar-upoko's young man waded through the brown water to the papyrus plant where Ulando was perching. He plunged his arms into the smelly, brown water. Desperately he swung his arms round, feeling nothing except slimy grass and roots like gooey jelly. Then he felt a face, an arm and another arm. Taking tight hold, he heaved and pulled, and pulled and heaved. Slowly, oozy-oozily a horrid heap of coiling, yukky weeds appeared. It dripped. It stank. It steamed in the sunlight.

Nyar-upoko.

Filthy and slimy, but alive and breathing. They brought her ashore and wiped off the worst of the muck.

And then – and then, EVERYBODY, including Ulando, the lark up in the sky, escorted Nyar-upoko back to the village, dancing and singing, and the women shrilling piercingly over it all:
'Yiri-yiri-yiri-yiiii. Yiri-yiri-yiri-yiiii.'

'Home she comes once more
          (Chorus) Jingle bells
from the dirty, swampy slime
          Jingle bells
lively as before, laughing all the time.
          Jingle bells
Dead we thought she was.
          Jingle bells
Ulando gave her life.
          Jingle bells
And now we're singing loud because she's going to be a wife: Wooo!

29

Jingle bells, jingle bells,
Jingle all the way.
Oh, what fun it is to bring
the girl back home today:
Wooo!'

In the village the young man's mother helped Nyar-upoko take a bath and gave her a new wrapper. The other nine young men went out together, back along the path to the forest to wait for the nine girls to come.

They came, each with a bundle of firewood on her head. The young men stopped them and shouted angrily:

'Clear off! Go on! Go back home!'

'You're causing us a lot of trouble here.'

'You and your jealousy. Go back to your own village.'

'We don't want murderers here.'

'Go on! Clear off!'

The nine girls dropped their bundles and ran off, screaming in fright.

A few weeks later the young man's family led eight fine cows to the village where Nyar-upoko's parents lived, as her bride-price. And the young man and Nyar-upoko were married."

Grandma is silent, puffing at her pipe. The dog is sleeping, curled up on its shadow. But the frogs and millions and trillions of busy *dudus* keep on with their stories, hidden in the grey bushes and the dark grey trees in the moonlight.

· 2 ·
Zazamankh

You know how long it seems from one Christmas to the next, don't you. . . ? . . .

Days follow days and it seems as if Christmas will never come, doesn't it. . . ? . . .

Well, something like five thousand Christmases ago . . . Yes, five thousand Christmases. Just think of that for a moment. Five years ago: you were still a bit of a baby then, weren't you? And ten times five is fifty: fifty years ago, that must be before your parents were born. And ten times fifty is five hundred: five hundred years ago, that must be about the time of your great-great-great-great-great-great — well, ever so uncountably great-grandparents. And ten times five hundred is five thousand: five thousand years ago, there can't have been anybody alive then, can there?

But there were. Lots of people were alive then, especially in Egypt. Clever and daft, busy and bored just like today. And one of them was King Sneferu, a Pharaoh, a king, living in his palace on the banks of the River Nile.

King Sneferu was King of the North and South, Victorious, King of Upper and Lower Egypt, living for all time, life, strength and health to him! That's what

31

the ancient Egyptians used to say to each other when they met: "Life, strength and health to you!"

King Sneferu lived in an immense palace, with halls and pillars, and paintings on the walls and servants and ministers and everything kings are supposed to have, including a lovely boating lake with grassy banks and beautiful papyrus plants with feathery tops, green and white, like fireworks exploding slowly overhead.

Well, one day five thousand years ago, his majesty King Sneferu – life, strength and health to him – was feeling depressed, bored. He couldn't think of anything he hadn't done many times before. There wasn't anything he wanted to do and he couldn't bear the thought of doing nothing. It was all so boring – so boring. You know what I mean. . . ? . . .

Yes, well, it happens to kings too.

So, he called together all his palace advisers and asked them to suggest something he could do, some fun and games that would cheer him up.

They suggested this; and they suggested that; and they suggested the other thing. But nothing appealed to the King of Upper and Lower Egypt. Boring: it was all just so boring.

So he said, "You lot don't know what fun is. Go and bring me my Chief Minister, Zazamankh."

Off the advisers went in different directions through this enormous palace, calling down the corridors between the tall pillars, "Zazamankh! Zazamankh!"

And louder, echoing, "ZAZAMANKH – ANKH! ZAZAMANKH – ANKHANKHANKH!"

"Your majesty requires my presence," said a quiet voice by King Sneferu's ear. And the shouting was still

32

going on: "ZAZAMANKH –ANKH! ZAZAMANKH – ANKHANKHANKH!"

"Ah! Here you are, Zazamankh, life, strength and health to you. How on earth did you get here? I didn't hear you come."

"I heard you say my name, your majesty; may you live for ever," said Zazamankh. "And I came as only I know how."

King Sneferu said, "I need cheering up. I called together all my ministers and asked them to suggest something. But all their ideas were so boring. I need a brainwave from you."

Zazamankh said, "If your majesty will go down to the lake of this great palace, you will see on the water the royal barge whose hull is made of cedar wood and seats of black ebony. The crew for this barge shall be the girls of the greatest beauty from the inner apartments of your palace. Then shall the heart of your majesty be uplifted as you see how the girls row back and forth on the surface of the lake. You shall see the pleasant nesting-places round your lake; you shall see its meadows and its lovely banks. Yes, I think the heart of your majesty will indeed be uplifted."

"A great idea," said King Sneferu. "That's just what I'll do. Now you go back to your house and I'll go boating."

The great King of the North and South called his palace attendants and said, "Bring me twenty oars, the ebony ones with cedarwood handles and blades inlaid with gold. And bring me twenty girls, those with the best legs, the finest breasts, and the nicest hair-dos; girls who haven't had any babies yet. And also bring

33

twenty fishnets and give the nets to the girls instead of
clothes."

And that's what they did, just as King Sneferu
wanted. He stepped into the barge with the twenty
girls and they rowed up and down the lake. And as they
rowed they sang:

> 'Here we go rowing his majesty,
> his majesty, his majesty.
> Here we go rowing his majesty,
> all on a holiday morning.'

You can sing this to the tune of Nuts in May

And that did the king a power of good, as you can
imagine. Cheered him up no end, it did, watching the
girls rowing and listening to them singing.

But then the leading girl on one side of the barge got tangled up in her own braided hair as she rowed. And her new pendant, a fish brooch made of green emerald, fell in the water. She didn't sing any more and stopped rowing. And the other nine girls on her side stopped rowing too, and the barge hit the bank.

His majesty King Sneferu said, "What's the matter? Don't you want to row any more?"

And the girls said, "It's our leader. She's not singing. She's stopped rowing."

So his majesty said to the girl, "Why aren't you rowing, my dear?"

And she said, "It's my new pendant, a fish brooch made of green emerald. It's fallen in the water."

So his majesty sent for another new pendant, a fish brooch made of green emerald, just like the girl's. And he said to the girl, "Here you are, my dear. I'm giving you this one instead."

But the girl said, "No! It's my own pendant I want. I don't want anything else. I want my pot right down to the bottom."

I'll let you into a little secret which even the editor and the wise professors don't know. Just imagine that at this moment you are in Africa, waiting for your supper. You might be gazing into the fire, listening to the cooking pot bubbling away, or watching your mother stirring the maize-flour porridge inside the pot. Porridge is nice. But the best bit of all is the crust which remains in the bottom of the pot after your mother has poured the porridge out. If you forgot your manners, you too might say: "I want my pot right down to the bottom."

"Great plagues of Nubia!" exclaimed the mighty Pharaoh, the King of Upper and Lower Egypt, King Sneferu Victorious, in frustration. And he called for Zazamankh: "Zazamankh! Zazamankh!"

"Your majesty requires my presence," said the quiet voice by King Sneferu's ear.

And they were still calling him up and down the palace.

"ZAZAMANKH! ZAZAMANKH – ANKH – ANKH! ZA. . ."

That's enough; he's here already.

King Sneferu said, "Ah! Here you are; life, strength and health to you for all time. Look, Zaza, my friend, can you help me? I've done exactly what you told me and it worked like a charm. I was cheered up no end as I watched these girls rowing. But this girl here lost her pendant in the water and she wouldn't row any more and she wouldn't take another pendant from me. She said – do you know what she said to me? She said, 'It's my own pendant I want. I want my pot right down to the bottom.' Hmph! She quite spoiled my fun. So, that's the problem. Her pendant's down there at the bottom of the lake. Can you do anything about it?"

Zazamankh, the Chief Minister, went down to the water's edge, and these are the magic words he said to the water:

𓀁𓄿𓂝𓏏𓏤𓈖𓏥 𓅱𓃀𓇋𓀗𓆱𓊪𓏏𓈖

And do you know what happened? One half of the water folded on top of the other half, just like a hinge. I kid you not; one half of the water just folded on top of

36

the other half. The water had been twelve arm-lengths deep at its deepest place, so, when it was folded, it was twenty-four arm-lengths deep. And there on a stone in the middle of the lake bed at the deepest spot was the girl's new pendant, the fish brooch made of green emerald.

Zazamankh walked out to the middle, brought the fish brooch back and gave it to the girl. Then he stood at the water's edge again and these are the magic words he said:

$$\text{𓀀 𓋴 𓇋 𓈖 𓅱 𓈖 𓈖 𓆛 𓊪 𓇾 𓏏 𓏤 𓈖}$$

And the water unfolded exactly as it had been before; exactly as before. Cross my heart and hope to die. The water unfolded right back as it had been before.

Well, King Sneferu, the mighty Pharaoh, the King of Upper and Lower Egypt was flabbergasted. Wordless, the great Pharaoh stood there; life, strength and health to him.

When at last King Sneferu recovered, he loaded Zazamankh with king-sized rewards, and continued his boating on the water.

The first magic spell sounds something like this:

"*Imee wen remen en moo en pa she her wau sen.*"

And the second spell sounds something like this:

"*Imee een too nah en moo en pa she er ahau sen.*"

It doesn't really matter how you pronounce these spells because nowadays nobody knows for sure how the ancient Egyptians pronounced their writing.

But suppose! Just suppose! Come on, you're not supposing.

Suppose that when you are saying the first spell, your mum's tea gets stacked up, one half on top of the other, in her cup, and inside you can see the bottom of half the cup.

Then, I'm telling you, THEN: you have just started AN ADVENTURE. Take hold of yourself, take a deep breath and don't try any more spells.

The first thing you must do is take a photo. You can send the photo to a newspaper and become famous for a day or two. But if you want to become famous for ever, like the Pharaohs – life, strength and health to them – you must phone the department of archaeology in the nearest university. Tell them you have just solved one of the mysteries of the Pharaohs; tell them you have discovered how to pronounce hieroglyphs and tell them what's happened to your mum's tea.

They won't believe you, of course, because people often speak to them about crackpot ideas like yours. But you must not give up if you want to become famous; not if you want to become really famous like a Pharaoh. Life, strength and health to you for all time!

•3•

The Man With a Tree on His Head

I expect you think it's always hot in Africa, don't
you. . . ? . . . Well, in some parts, way down in the
south, they have winter and it gets cold at night. The
leaves fall off the trees, everything stops growing and
there are no insects. You have to wrap up well because
sometimes there's a frost at night.

It's chilly tonight. Not cold enough for frost yet, but
there's a fire out in the courtyard. There's no moon,
but the stars are up there in the black sky – millions of
tiny, silent pinholes flung all over the black hood of
night.

And here comes Grandma shuffling outside into the
courtyard. She sits with her feet towards the fire and
pulls a blanket round her shoulders to keep her back
warm. She picks up a long branch and pushes one end
of it into the fire. A flame flares out and sparks shoot
up to join the stars overhead.

In the light of the flame you can see the round house
with its overhanging thatch and the low wall that
surrounds the clean-swept courtyard. The wall and the
house are painted with patterns of squares and circles,
and over the door you can read BLESS THIS HOUSE.

Inside the house there are sounds of people working.

40

There's always work to be done and Mother does most of it. Her children, Tebogo and his little sister, Tshipidi, help as much as they can. But inside the house it's always Mother who cooks, washes and cleans. And outside the house it's always Mother who does most of the digging, weeding and harvesting of the crops.

When Mother and the children have finished their jobs inside the house, they come out carrying blankets, one for the children and one for Mother. They sit down side by side with their feet towards the fire next to Grandma, and wrap the blankets right round themselves and in a peak over their heads. From behind they look like small tents. It's chilly tonight, nippy on the nose and ears.

Tebogo is twelve years old and is proud of the English he's learnt at school. He likes to teach his little sister, Tshipidi, who's only seven.

"Good morning. How are you?" he says.

"Goomorring. Ow ow you?" Tshipidi repeats and Tebogo tries to correct her.

Sometimes she says "Goomorring" in the evening, but Tebogo doesn't correct her because his English lessons are always in the morning, so he hasn't learnt to say "Good afternoon" or "Good evening".

"Grandma," says Tebogo, "I can see a long story stick in the fire. Are you going to tell us a long story tonight?"

"No," says Grandma, "you know all my stories. Your mother can tell you a different story tonight."

Overhead, the pinhole stars are twinkling, and beyond the courtyard wall the shapes of flat-topped thorn trees flicker in the firelight, white, like trees in a negative.

Mother says, "All right then, I'll tell you about the man with a tree on his head. But it won't be a long story. It's getting cold and I'm tired. So we'll burn the branch quickly and make the story short.

This man was selfish and lazy. He used to do a little work and then say he'd finished. Then he used to go to sleep. So his wife had to do most of the work at the lands, all the cooking in the house, look after the cattle and goats and the children, and do many other jobs besides. Her life was hard but she had to work because he was stronger than she was and, if she didn't work, he'd hit her.

Well, it's said that one morning this man woke up to find a tree growing out of the top of his head, a lovely *mopané* tree with whispery leaves. The tree was lovely to look at but it certainly wasn't lovely to wear on your head. Just imagine a tree on your head. You couldn't turn your head quickly or you'd spin like a top, wouldn't you?

> "And you couldn't bend down,"
> says Tebogo, "because the tree
> would pull you
> down to the ground."
> "That's right," says Mother. "And
> imagine going through doors.
> You'd have to crouch right down,
> keeping your back straight."

42

> "And the squirrels and birds would come," says Tshipidi, "birds and birds and birds and birds and they'd all make messes in your hair."
> "They would indeed," says Mother, and she pushes a bit more of the story branch into the fire.

Well, anyway, the man didn't like it one bit. 'Wife! Wife!' he bellowed. 'Come here at once.'

His wife came into the room and saw the tree on her husband's head. She gasped and clapped her hands to her cheeks. Then she began to sing:

'Husband mine!
What's that strange thing I can see that's grown upon your head?
grown upon your head?
grown upon your head?
grown upon your head?
What's that strange thing I can see . . .'

'Stop that silly noise AT ONCE!' her husband said. 'I don't need you to make a song of it. I need you to pull it off. Come on, pull! Pull!'

'But husband,' she said, 'it's not for me to take it away. It's a job for an African doctor.'

'Pull it off, I said. At once!'

So, to calm her husband and prove to him that she couldn't pull the tree off, she took hold of a branch and gave a good tug.

'Aaaah! Ow wowowow!' Her husband roared in pain

and anger. 'Wife! Wife! That's not the way to do it. Don't yank like that. Pull steadily. Don't you know how to pull trees up yet?'

So, she got hold of the branch again and pulled hard and steadily. Heeeave!

Come on, once more. All together now.

HEEAVE! And again. HEEEAVE! And again . . .
'Stop! STOP!' yelled the man. 'That's not the way to do it. Do you want to pull my brains out and make me as foolish as you? Go and bring the saw AT ONCE!'

So she went off and came back with a saw and started sawing the trunk of the tree. But she made only one cut.

'Aaaah! Ow! OW WOWOWOW! It's me you're cutting,' yelled the man. And sure enough some blood was coming out of the trunk.

'What you need is an African doctor,' she said.

'Don't talk rubbish, woman,' said her husband. 'What do African doctors know with all their bones and abracadabra? Bring the cart and take me to hospital at once. The white doctors can cure this.'

So she hitched two donkeys to the cart, helped her husband into the back and drove off to hospital.

Clip-clop-clippy-clop. Clip-clop-clippy-clop.
Clip-clop-clippy clop. Clip-clop-clippy-clop.
Gee up there! Go on drive the donkeys.

And the *mopané* tree on the man's head:

Sss-wish. Sss-wish. Sss-wish. Sss-wish.
Gee up there! Keep those donkeys going, lazy beasts. That's right. All the way to the hospital.

Whoa there! Wo! Wo! Woo! We're at the hospital now.

In the waiting room the man ignored all the other people who'd been there for hours and walked straight into the doctor's room. He sat on the floor and said to the doctor, '*Drumela mma.* You see my problem, doctor.'

'*Dumela rra,*' said the doctor, who was white. 'Yes, this is a most unusual phenomenon.'

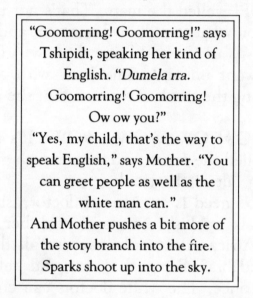

"Goomorring! Goomorring!" says Tshipidi, speaking her kind of English. "*Dumela rra.* Goomorring! Goomorring! Ow ow you?"
"Yes, my child, that's the way to speak English," says Mother. "You can greet people as well as the white man can."
And Mother pushes a bit more of the story branch into the fire. Sparks shoot up into the sky.

So the white doctor looked down the man's throat, took his temperature, tapped his knee and finally called in the other white doctors. They all stood around, with their hands in the pockets of their white coats, talking in their difficult doctor's language. The man thought he could hear them saying words like 'folosh' and 'dendro' and 'pidry rhubarb' and 'cephali'. Finally one of the doctors said, 'Yes, this is a severe case of dendro-cephali-carcino-genesis.'

'What?' said the man.

'Dendrocephalicarcinogenesis,' replied the doctor.

'Most interesting. Anyway, this hospital is too small; it's not possible for this ailment to be treated here. An appointment has been made for this phenomenon to be examined in Johannesburg. Goodbye.'

'I have dendro-whats-it,' said the man to his wife. 'And they've made an appointment for me in Johannesburg. What nonsense! How can I go to Johannesburg in a donkey cart? It would take us a week. Take me to the African doctor at once.'

'Yes, my husband. Good idea,' said the wife. And she drove off to the African doctor's house, smiling to herself a little bit.

Clip-clop-clippy-clop. Clip-clop-clippy-clop.

Gee up there! Get a move on. And don't forget the tree.

That's right. Nearly there now.

47

Whoa! Wo! Wo! We're at the African doctor's house now, and there's the doctor herself, waiting outside for us.

'*Dumela rra. Dumela mma,*' said the doctor. 'I was expecting you to come earlier. Come inside, please.'

So they went inside the house and sat down.

'Well now,' said the doctor, 'I know what's caused this tree to grow on your head. You men are too harsh. You're cheating us women badly. We're being killed by all this work. But things are changing and you must change too. I can cure you, but it'll cost you a cow.'

'I don't care what it costs,' said the man. 'Just get rid of this tree and I'll pay you a cow as soon as my cows come home from grazing tonight.'

So the doctor stood over him as he sat on the ground, put her hands on the tree and sang her curing song.

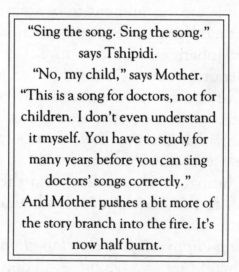

"Sing the song. Sing the song."
says Tshipidi.
"No, my child," says Mother.
"This is a song for doctors, not for children. I don't even understand it myself. You have to study for many years before you can sing doctors' songs correctly."
And Mother pushes a bit more of the story branch into the fire. It's now half burnt.

And as she sang, the tree slowly became smaller and smaller and smaller and vanished. And the man was back to normal again with nothing but his hair on his head.

The man was very happy. 'Wife! Wife! Take me home AT ONCE!' And off he went in the cart without even saying thank you to the doctor.

Gee up there!

Clip-clop-clippy-clop. Clip-clop-clippy-clop.

But no tree noise this time. Remember?

Two months passed and the man didn't pay the cow to the doctor. So the African doctor thought to herself, 'I'll send a messenger to remind him to pay me the cow.' And she called the birds from the trees.

First, she spoke to the finch, Mantsi-motsimo: 'If I send you, my child, what will you say to the man?'

'I'll say "Tsimo! Tsimo! Tsimo!"' said Mantsi-motsimo.

'No, no, that won't do,' said the African doctor. 'I won't send you.' And she turned to the pigeon, Lenkuru-kuru: 'And what about you, Lenkuru-kuru, my child, what'll you say?'

'I'll say "Kuru-kuruuu! Kuru-kuruuu!"' said Lenkuru-kuru.

'No, no, that won't do at all. I won't send you, either,' said the doctor. And she turned to the dove, Rankwi-dingwane. 'And what about you, Rankwi-dingwane, my dear, what'll you say?'

Rankwi-dingwane, the dove said, 'This is what I'll sing:

Listen here, listen here,
tree man.
Wasn't it a tree on your head,

tree man?
Wasn't it me who made you well,
tree man?
Wasn't it a promise that you made,
tree man?
Wasn't it a cow that you promised,
tree man?
Listen here, listen here,
tree man.
Wasn't it a . . .'

The doctor was very pleased and said to the dove, 'Yes, my child, you can take the message.'

So, Rankwi-dingwane, the dove, flew to where the man was sleeping. She perched on a tree near him and sang her song.

The man woke up in alarm when he heard the dove and he shouted out, 'Hey! I'm being bewitched. What for? These words can bewitch people. Shoo! Go on, clear off!' And he waved his arms at the dove and ran off to find his wife.

'Wife! Wife!' he shouted. 'Come here. I'm being bewitched by a bird.'

'What does it say to bewitch you?' she asked when she met him.

But before he could answer, they heard the dove singing from the wall around the courtyard of their house.

'Hey! Hey!' shouted the man. 'I'm being bewitched. Shoo!' And he picked up a stick and threw it. The dove flew off.

Mother pushes the story branch
further into the fire. "Right," she
says, "it's getting colder and
colder. We'll finish
the story quickly and
go inside to bed."
And they all move closer to the
flickering fire and wrap their
blankets tighter
round themselves.

Rankwi-dingwane flew back to the African doctor and told her all that had happened. The doctor was angry, as you might expect.

The next morning – well, the next morning I'm sure you can guess what happened to the man, can't you. . . ? . . .

Yes, the tree was back again on his head, the lovely *mopané* tree with whispery leaves. His wife could see it growing bigger and bigger. 'Husband, dear! The tree! The tree! It's back again. You've been bewitched.'

'Yes, yes, I don't need you to tell me that, woman,' said the man angrily. 'Shut up and listen! Send someone to call that woman here to take the tree away. AT ONCE!'

So a young girl ran from his house to the doctor's house and said to the doctor, 'The man with the tree on his head says you're to go to his house at once.'

And the doctor said to the young girl, 'Go to his house? Tell him I will not go to him. He must come to me. And tell him also that, when he comes, he must bring two cows, one for the first healing and another for the second.'

51

The young girl returned to the man's house and told the man with the tree on his head what the doctor had said. So, there was nothing for it. They had to bring two cows. They hitched the donkeys to the cart, loaded the man into the back and set off for the doctor's house.

Gee up there! Gee up!

Clip-clop-clippy-clop. Clip-clop-clippy-clop.

And this time the *mopané* tree on his head whispered in the breeze as they drove along:

Selfish. Selfish. Selfish. Selfish.

When they reached the doctor's house – the two donkeys, the cart, the man and his wife, the two cows and the cowherd – the doctor was waiting for them.

'If you'd changed your ways sooner,' she said, 'you wouldn't be in this mess now. For too long now, men have been people loved by God. We women have put up with it because it was our job and it was easier that way. But it's time now for us women to share a bit of God's love too. We're beginning to see we're being cheated. I hope that this time you'll remember.'

She put her hands on the man's head and sang her doctor's song again. The tree slowly – slowly – faded – faded and vanished. The man's head was like other men's heads.

'Thank you,' said the man. 'Here are your cows.'

And after that his wife thought her life began to seem a little bit less hard – just a little bit."

The story branch is completely burnt out now.

"Come on, everybody," says Mother. "the story's finished. It's cold. Let's go to bed now."

So they take their blankets and go inside, leaving the glowing fire and the millions of stars overhead.

· 4 ·

The Bag Of Money

Plock-drip-drip-drip. Plock-drip-drip-drip.
Plock-drip-drip-drip.
Salim is a very careful young boy tonight, sitting
there at the back of the long dug-out canoe, paddling
us all across the river. It's the first time he's been
allowed to take the canoe out at night. But tonight's a
special occasion. The famous *griot*, Ibrahim Kan, is
telling stories in the village on the other side. He
comes every year after the harvest when everybody has
time to relax, especially if the harvest's been good.
And this year the harvest has been good.
Plock-drip-drip-drip. Plock-drip-drip-drip.
Plock-drip-drip-drip.
In fact, it isn't difficult to paddle tonight. There are
two moons and it's almost as bright as day. One moon
is round and steady up there overhead; the other moon
is a shimmering line, leading straight across the water
to the canoe. All the same, Salim's paddling his canoe
very carefully. We're quite a canoeful; Salim's mother
and father, his young sister, Fatuma, baby Malik, two
or three aunts and uncles, one grandad, several cousins
and us.
When the canoe reaches the other bank, we all get

54

out and walk slowly up the path. The air hums and burps with the all-night concert of insects and frogs. Sometimes, for no reason I know of, they all stop and the silence is frightening. It's like waiting with bated breath for the end of the world. But then the concert continues and we're no longer alone in the world.

We come to a large group of people sitting round a man on a stool under the silk-cotton tree in the middle of the village. We sit down with the crowd and greet our friends and they greet us: "*Salaam aleikum.*"

"*Aleikum salaam.*"

Ibrahim Kan has just finished telling a story. It must have been that funny one about the stupid hyena who fought a monster, a *konderong*, and kept on losing when the *konderong* threw him to the ground. Some children are still practising the noise of the hyena hitting the ground: "krram-bam-bum-tumble-biffy-biff-slap-slap! Krrram-bam-bum-tumble-biffy-biff-slap-slap!"

Ibrahim Kan clears his throat and begins the next tale in the traditional way: "There was a tale."

"Our legs are crossed," we all reply.

"It happened here."

"It was so."

"There was a man who married a woman. And the day he brought his wife home was the last day he had any money or happiness for a long time. Sometimes when his wife cooked, she refused to bring him any food; all he had was the smell of it. Sometimes she beat him till he cried and ran away into his house. She was tough, that wife. She never gave him any money from her harvesting and trading, so he was ashamed to visit

his friends because he had no money to buy them anything. And anyway, sometimes she even refused to let him leave his own compound.

The years passed and the husband became thoroughly miserable. Not even the birth of three sons cheered him up because the sons helped their mother, not their father. If they earned any money, they used to share it with their mother.

One day the husband decided things had gone far enough. He decided he would leave home and go out into the world to see what he could find. So that night, when everybody was asleep, he crept out of his house and went to town where he had just one friend.

The husband said, 'My friend, I've had just about enough of that wife of mine. I don't know where I'm going, but I'm off to see what I can find. When you go to see my wife tomorrow, just tell her I've gone.' And he went.

The next morning the friend went to see the man's wife. When he entered the compound he asked her, 'Where's your husband?'

'How should I know? I haven't seen him,' she said.

'Well,' said the friend, 'he's gone on a long journey.'

'Good riddance,' she said. 'I hope he dies there.'

The husband travelled around for a year in search of money. But by the end of the year he'd found nothing except a one *damasi* coin, given him one day by a stranger. He looked at this one *damasi* coin in his hand and wondered what on earth he could do.

But as he sat there wondering – God be praised, he had a brain-wave. God put a wonderful idea in his head, and he stood up.

First, he found a piece of thin cloth and made a sack. Then he started making money. Well, not money really. You know those thin pots we use as water jars and how easily they get broken? Well, the husband went round collecting all those broken pieces. Then he sat down and started cutting them into coin-sized pieces, using his one *damasi* coin as a measure. It took him a whole month before he had a sackful. When the sack was full, he put the coin inside on the top, tied the sack up tight and set off home. With the pottery coins sticking into the thin cloth, it looked as if the sack was full of real coins.

It was night when he reached home. He went quietly into his house, shut the door, put the sack by his bed and went to sleep.

Early next morning he opened his door and sat on

his bed to wait. The first son to get up noticed his father's door was open. He crept up to the door, peered round and was surprised to see his father sitting on the bed.

The son didn't say anything but went straight to his mother and said, 'Mother!'

'Mmm?'

'Father's back.'

'Back?'

'Yes, he's sitting on his bed.'

'Let him die there,' said the wife. 'Who asked him to come back?'

The husband heard this but he waited and, after a while when nobody had come to see him in his house, he called one of his sons: 'Son!'

'Mmm?'

'Go and buy me some kola nuts.' And the father untied the sack and gave the coin to his son.

'Half a *damasi*,' said the father.

The son went to the market and bought half a *damasi* worth of kola nuts. The husband broke one of the nuts in half and said to the son, 'Take this half to your mother.'

The son said, 'And what about the change?'

'Keep it.'

The son went to his mother and gave her the half kola nut from her husband. The woman was very surprised because her husband had never ever given her a kola nut before, although it's our custom to give nuts.

The son said, 'He has a sack full of money. He took out a coin and told me to keep the change.'

'A sack full of money?' said the wife.

'Mmm!'

'So, that's the game, is it?' she said. And she sat and thought for a while. Then she stood up, went to her husband's house and greeted him: '*Salaam aleikum.*'

'*Aleikum salaam.* How's the family?' he replied.

'They're fine,' she said. 'You've been gone a long time.'

'Mmm!'

Then she went back to her house and thought again. She went out and killed one of her chickens. She cooked it to perfection with all the best herbs and spices. When it was ready, she took the chicken to her husband's house, knelt before him and presented him with the chicken. Then she went to fetch water for him to wash his hands.

The husband ate till he was full. Then he called his wife and she came and took away the dirty dish and water. The husband sat back on his bed and said to himself:

> Praise be to God, God is great.
> I've had a long time to wait.
> Not once in my life
> did I eat food from my wife.
> Now it's chicken and spice
> and many things nice.
> Praise be to God. God is great.

At lunch time his wife killed and cooked another chicken just as before. And for dinner there was still another chicken for him.

Just before bedtime the husband called his sons to his house and said to them, 'Before I left here, I saw you with a sack of cement. Is it still here?'

'Yes.'

'Bring it here and bring a spade too.'

The sons brought the cement and spade.

The father said, 'Move my bed over there.' And they moved it. 'Now dig a deep hole.'

When the hole was dug, the father lifted the sack very carefully, pretending it was heavy, and put it in the hole. Then he said, 'Now put the earth back and cover it with cement. Then put my bed back.' And for the first time in their lives the sons did exactly as their father told them.

When they had finished, the father said, 'Now sit down and listen. Ever since I was born I've had no money, but I've always dreamed of having money to leave to my family after I die. Now God has granted my wish. When I was away, God helped me find this sack of money. The money is there. I will not take a coin from it and you will not take a coin from it either. But when I die the money will be yours to share among yourselves. Now go to bed.'

The sons went to their mother and she asked them, 'What did he call you for?'

They said, 'In the name of God, our father has a big sack of money.' And they told their mother what they had just done.

The mother said, 'Your father has been spoken to by God. We must take good care of your father. The way we used to treat him will now stop. We will take care of him till he dies.'

And so it was. Sometimes it was chicken he ate. But the wife also had an unending supply of sheep and goats. If her husband breakfasted on chicken, he would dine on lamb. And his clothes were made of material of the best quality because his wife even bought him the material. He lived a good life and became fat as he sat around his house all day.

And that was all he did, till one day he became very ill. His wife nursed him and brought him every small thing he needed till finally he died.

The eldest son called his two brothers and said, 'Our father is dead. We spent all our money on him when he was alive, but we must let people know that we are now men of property. We must have a big feast at his funeral. I will borrow a bull to provide meat for the feast. Whatever they charge me I will agree to. I will pay back when we have buried our father and dug up the sack of money.'

The second son said, 'And I will borrow a sack of rice and pay back when I receive my share of our father's money.'

The youngest son said, 'And I will borrow the tomatoes, onions and oil. And I too will pay back when I receive my share.'

And that's what they did. They borrowed everything they needed. The feast was prepared. The guests came and ate till they were full. The father was buried and all the guests went back home.

That night the sons went to their father's house with picks and spades. They locked the door and lit the lamp. They moved his bed and began to dig till they came to the sack. They untied the sack, held it upside down, poured everything out and looked in disbelief.

'In the name of God, what's this?' said the youngest son.

'God have mercy on us,' said the second son. 'What has our father done to us?'

The eldest son said, 'And what are we going to do with the people we have borrowed the bull, the rice, the tomatoes, the onions and the oil from? What are we going to do with our father? We must take him out of his grave and beat him.'

And that won't do any good, will it?"

Ibrahim Kan finishes his tale and says, "Well, what do you think? Was she a good wife? Was he a good husband? Were they good sons?"

And then there starts a discussion, so long and so hot we are afraid we won't be able to cross the river before the moon goes down.

So we leave and discuss the questions ourselves as we go down the path to the river.

We all get into the canoe and Salim paddles us carefully back home among the moons and the unending concert of insects and frogs.

Plock-drip-drip. Plock-drip-drip.

And when we reach the other side we still haven't agreed on answers to any of the questions.

Can you agree . . . ? . . .

· 5 ·

The Good Herdboy

There's a lovely house in Africa where two boys and
a girl live. Joseph's twelve, Rosemary's ten and
Peter's seven. They all go to a primary school on the
other side of the River Garagoli which rushes fast over
a little waterfall behind the house. Below the waterfall
an enormous tree trunk lies across the river. That's the
short cut to school. But if the Garagoli's in flood, the
water comes over the tree trunk and the children have
to take the much longer way to school along the roads.

In front of the house is a small verandah, a lawn,
some flowers, a road and then some gigantic trees –
eucalyptus trees with long tisselly-tasselly leaves. The
trees are beautiful and have a lovely smell. But monkeys live in them, colobus monkeys with long, black and
white hair draped on their backs like Grandma's shawl.
These monkeys are a nuisance because they come and
eat the maize that grows behind the house.

When the children aren't at school, or doing jobs for
their mother, they spend a lot of time helping the dog
chase the monkeys out of the maize. Well, that's what
they're supposed to be doing, but I know – and they
know I know – that often they aren't chasing monkeys;
that's a dog's job.

Often Joseph and Peter are down at the Garagoli making toy water-mills like the real water-mills along the river that grind the maize into flour. And Rosemary? I know that often she's in one of the neighbour's houses helping to look after their babies.

But in the evenings after sunset, when the moon is up, Joseph, Rosemary, Peter and their friends and I sit on the verandah at the front of the house, and I tell them stories, stories we tell children in my country.

One moonlit night I remember starting to tell the story of Rapunzel, but the dog starts growling and runs off into the moonlight towards the gate. He has very sharp ears their dog has. I can only hear the water in the Garagoli, the night insects and some drums in the distance, drumming for an all night wedding party:

Doom-de. Doom-de. Doom-de. Doom-de.
Doom-de. Doom-de.

But the dog soon comes back, wagging his tail and we see the dark shape of a man in the moonlight.

"It's Mr Sabwa," shout the children. "*Milembé muno.*"

And that's the end of my story. Mr Sabwa's a very famous story-teller. He's even been on the radio – several times. And here he is. He's all dressed up with his monkey skin hat on his head and a beautiful long-haired colobus skin cloak. And he has his *ishiriri*, his fiddle, too.

"Tell us a story, Mr Sabwa, please," the children beg him. Rosemary and Joseph run into the house for a stool for Mr Sabwa to sit on and a bottle of beer to bring the story out.

"Well," says Mr Sabwa, his white eyes and teeth

gleaming in the moonlight. "I'm really on my way to that wedding. You can hear the drums over there. But that party'll go on all night, so it doesn't matter if I'm a bit late. And I know that in this house stories find a good home. So I'll tell you one story."

Mr Sabwa sits down on the stool and takes a big swig of beer from the bottle. "I'll tell you the story of the good herdboy. You boys know all about herding cattle, don't you?"

"Yes, Mr Sabwa," say the boys.

"And we girls know one or two things about cattle too," says Rosemary.

"Yes," says Mr Sabwa, "times are changing. Some girls these days know more about herding than boys do. But in the old days, when this story was first told, it was only boys who did the herding.

Well then, a long time ago there was a great famine and there was nothing to eat in this land. A man was walking home through the forest when he came across a small boy – a small, frightened boy, hungry, lost and very dirty. The man picked the boy up and took him home and gave him to the eldest of his three wives to look after.

And he said to his three wives, 'This boy's mine. I'm the one who brought him into the family. Look after him well. When he's big enough, he'll look after my cattle.'

As the years passed, he grew to be a fine young boy and he started going with the other boys, learning how to herd cattle. When he was properly grown up and responsible – not sciving off to make water-mills by the

river like some of you whose names I won't mention but we all know who they are, don't we? Well, when he was responsible, the man let him take the cattle to the grazing ground by himself.

It was a big job because the man owned a lot of cattle. But the boy did it well. He loved the cattle and spent all his time with them. The cattle grew fat and breathed their warm contented breath over him when he pulled the ticks off their hides. Every day the boy would take them off to the river to drink, and then find the best grass for grazing. In the evening he'd take them to drink again and then bring them home. Some of the cattle slept outside, others had their own sheds. But the leader of them all, the glossy black bull with shoulders billowing like thunderclouds, this bull slept in the house of the senior wife, where the boy also slept.

Now, one day at the evening meal the adults started talking about a strange man who'd appeared in the area, a man from a far off country who couldn't remember his home.

The boy laughed and said, 'Why couldn't he remember his home? I left my home when I was a little boy and I can still remember it.'

The adults were very surprised and the father said, 'That's not your home. This is your home.'

The boy said, 'If I go towards where the sun rises and follow that line of hills, I'll reach my home.'

The man was shocked and said, 'But how can you remember that place?'

The boy answered, 'I can remember how you brought me here when I was a tiny boy.'

The man thought the boy was lying; he thought somebody had told him. 'You'd better go off to bed now,' the man said. 'This is your home.'

"And it's time for little Peter to go to bed too," says Mr Sabwa.
All the children look round – there's a large crowd of children here tonight. And we see Peter fast asleep. Rosemary picks Peter up and carries him into the house. "He's made too many water-mills today, I bet," says Mr Sabwa and he takes a long drink from his bottle of beer.

Well, when the boy was asleep, the man asked his wives, 'Who told the boy where he came from? Did you . . . ? . . .

'No.'

'Did you . . . ? . . .'

'No.'

'Did you . . . ? . . .'

'No.'

'Hmph!' said the man. 'Is all that food we've given him, all the clothes, all the care we've taken of him – is it all for nothing? Are we just going to sit back and watch my boy walk out of that door and not come back after all the trouble we've taken?'

One of the women said, 'We could put poison in his soup tomorrow. When he drinks it, he'll die.'

And that's what they agreed to do – put poison in the boy's soup the next day.

But all this time the glossy black bull in his dark corner of the house was chewing his cud:

Tut – tut – tut – tut – tut – tut

and listening, listening and thinking, 'They're going to kill my excellent herdboy. Then who'll look after me and my cows? Mmmm! By my horns I swear I'll not let this happen.'

Tut – tut – tut – tut – tut – tut.

So the next day, when it was time for the boy to bring the cattle back home, the bull went up to the boy and began to sing:

Mr Sabwa picks up his bottle and shakes it; it's empty. Joseph runs inside for another bottle of beer.

69

> Mr Sabwa picks up his *ishiriri* and
> says, "We'll sing this together; I'm
> the bull, you're the boy." Joseph
> returns with a new bottle.
> Mr Sabwa takes a swig and begins
> to play his *ishiriri*.

'Herdboy, will you tell on me, herdboy?'
    'Never will I tell.'
'Hot soup, don't you drink it up, hot soup.'
    'Never will I tell.'
'Cold milk, that's the food for you, cold milk.'
    'Never will I tell.'
'Herdboy, will you tell on me, herdboy?'
    'Never will I tell.'

So the boy took the cattle back home and put them in
their sleeping places – the bull in the senior wife's
house. When it was time to eat, the senior wife put
soup in front of the boy.

'I don't want hot soup tonight. I want cold milk,
please,' said the boy.

The wife took the soup away and brought him milk.
He drank it all up and then went to sleep.

The man was angry and called a second meeting in
the senior wife's house.

'Who told the boy about the soup? Did you . . . ?
. . .'

'No.'

'Did you . . . ? . . .'

'No.'

'Did you . . . ? . . .'

'No.'

'Well, tomorrow,' said the man, 'we'll put poison in everything. Then he'll surely die.'

Tut – tut – tut – mmmm – tut –tut –tut.

So the next day, when it was time for the boy to bring the cattle back home, the bull went up to him again and began to sing:

> Mr Sabwa takes another long drink
> from his bottle. "Mmm!" he says,
> "No poison in that. That bull had
> brains. He wasn't all muscle; he
> was a champion."
> Then he takes up his *ishiriri* and
> his bow and begins to play.

'Herdboy, will you tell on me, herdboy?'
'Never will I tell.'
'Cold milk, don't you drink it up, cold milk.'
'Never will I tell.'
'Fresh fruit, that's the food for you, fresh fruit.'
'Never will I tell.'
'Herdboy, will you tell on me, herdboy?'
'Never will I tell.'

The boy took the cattle back home and put them in their sleeping places – the bull in the senior wife's house as usual. When it was time to eat, the senior wife put some soup in front of the boy.

'I don't want any soup tonight,' said the boy.

'Well, let me bring you some cold milk,' said the wife.

71

'No, I don't feel like milk either. Bring me some fresh fruit from the garden, please.'

So she went into the garden and picked some pineapples and pears and put them in front of him. He ate them all up and then went to sleep.

The man was furious that the plan had failed again. They'd never thought of poisoning the fruit in the garden. So the man called a third meeting in the senior wife's house.

'Who told the boy there was poison in everything, did you . . . ? . . .'

'No.'

'Did you . . . ? . . .'

'No.'

'Did you . . . ? . . .'

'No.'

'Then search the house. Someone's listening. But quietly or you'll wake the boy. Is the boy asleep?'

They looked; he was. They searched the house, but, of course, nobody else was there. Only the great, black bull in his corner with his eyes shut, chewing:

Tut – tut – tut – tut – tut – tut – mmmm.

And it never occurred to them that the bull was listening. Well, it wouldn't, would it? You didn't think of it till I told you, did you. . . ? . . .

'All right, then,' said the man. 'Tomorrow we'll put some poison, magicked specially for him, in the gateway. When he passes through in the evening, he'll fall down and die. We can't fail this time.'

Tut – tut – tut – tut – mmmm – tut – tut – tut.

The next day, when it was time for the boy to bring the cattle back home, the bull went up to the boy again

72

and began to sing:

'Herdboy, will you tell on me, herdboy?'
'Never will I tell.'
'Gateway, don't you pass through there, gateway.'
'Never will I tell.'
'Hedgeway, that's the way for you, hedgeway.'
'Never will I tell.'
'Herdboy, will you tell on me, herdboy?'
'Never will I tell.'

The boy took the cattle back home. But when they went through the gateway, he pushed his way through the hedge that surrounded the compound; and he came to no harm. Then he put the cattle back in their sleeping places – the great, black bull, as usual, in the senior wife's house.

When it was time to eat, the senior wife brought him hot soup, and cold milk, and fresh fruit; and he ate it all up. And again he came to no harm. Then he went to sleep.

Well! Well, as you can imagine, the man and his wives were amazed. The man called a fourth meeting in the senior wife's house, and one of the wives stayed by the boy to check that he really was asleep all the time.

'This time we'll fix him good and proper,' the man said. 'We'll put poison for him in everything, in all his food and drink, in the gateway and all round the hedge, and in his bed. This has gone on long enough. Tomorrow will be that boy's last day on earth.'

Tut – tut – tut – tut – mmmm – tut – tut.

That night the bull didn't sleep; he was so worried about his good herdboy.

The next day the boy took the cattle grazing as usual, but the bull was obviously upset and didn't graze at all well. It kept raising its head and gazing at the boy with sad, sad eyes. The boy noticed his bull wasn't grazing properly and thought to himself, 'Last night Bull must have heard really terrible things.'

About midday, long before it was time to go home, the great, black bull, with tears pouring from his eyes, walked up to the boy and sang in a slow, deep, very sad, bull-toned voice:

'Herdboy, will you tell on me, herdboy?'
                  Never will I tell.'
'This way, don't you pass this way, this way.'
                  Never will I tell.'
'That way, that's the way for you, that way.'
                  Never will I tell.'
'Herdboy, will you tell on me, herdboy?'
                  Never will I tell.'

And all the time it was singing, great tears were rolling down the bull's face. The bull told the boy to climb on his back, and then the sad bull, still weeping, carried him off, following the line of hills towards the sunrise place, to his home, his real home where he'd been born many years before and where he'd be safe with his real parents.

When the boy had climbed down outside his home, the downcast bull turned round and trudged back to the cows. He rounded them up by himself and took them back to the man's compound – late, very late in the evening.

In the compound the man and his wives were arguing loud enough for the whole world to hear.

'That useless boy, he's run away with all my cattle.'

'Well, why didn't you kill him with a knife, like a real man does?'

'You were the ones who told him about the poison. How can I marry more wives if I have no cattle?'

And just then the bull arrived with all the cows. That put an end to the argument and they never mentioned the boy again.

But in the sunrise house they were preparing an all-night party to celebrate the lost child who returned a full grown man. The young man's mother, who as a young woman had shared her body with him, given him life and milk, now as an old woman gave birth again to a man.

Yiri-yiri-yiri-yiiii. Yiri-yiri-yiri-yiiii."

"That's it. That's all I'm telling you tonight," says Mr Sabwa. He finishes off his beer.

"Tell us another. Go and bring him another bottle."

Mr Sabwa grins and plays a few twiddly bits on his fiddle. "No, I've got to go to that wedding now."

He straightens his monkey hat, pulls the colobus cloak round his shoulders and strides off into the moonlight.

· 6 ·

Karimirwa and Musiguku

It's so dark tonight you can't see in front of your nose. It's like looking back inside your own skull. Nothing: except the stars overhead, a star for each story, millions of storyholes in your skull.

Away out there in the darkness, on the other side of our valley a fire is flickering and some shapes are moving round it.

"Look! Grandma's lit a fire outside."

"Do you think she's going to tell a story?" asks Grace.

"I should think so."

"Will you take us tonight, Tony?" asks Peter.

"Go and get a torch."

A minute later Grace and Peter come back, flashing the torch and we set off for Grandma's.

We go along the footpath down the hill, our ears drilled by the noise of crickets in the hedges.

"Tony, why's it cold down here?" asks Grace.

"Don't they tell you at school that hot air rises and cold air sinks? Careful now, it's a bit squidgy down here."

"Ugh! Look, Tony! There's a frog. Bring a stick," says Peter.

77

"No, don't do that. Leave it alone. It's doing you no harm," says Tony.

We walk on past the banana grove and we hear the huge banana leaves rustling and rattling against each other overhead. Then we come to the stream.

"Careful now. See the stepping stones? Oops! Ah well, never mind. You can dry your feet by the fire." We climb the slope on the other side.

"Doesn't that tea smell good?" On the slope on our left the torch beam lights up a green carpet of tea bushes, plucked smooth by the teapickers.

"*Woy*! Tony! Something's hit me. Something hairy," screams Peter.

There in the torch beam we see a donkey, standing right in the middle of the path.

"Ooo! It's scary, walking when it's dark like this. You can't see anything at all. Aren't you afraid of the dark, Tony?"

"Me? Afraid of the dark? No, I'm grown up. Look! There's Grandma's fire. And there are already lots of people here to listen to Grandma's stories."

We squeeze in, sit down and greet everybody.

"*Milembé*, Grandma!"

"*Milembé*, Tony! *Milembé*, Grace! *Milembé*, Peter! You're just in time for the next story," says Grandma. She puts another stick on the fire and flames shoot up. Shapes loom and flicker round us in the firelight – ugly shapes, scary shapes, now you see them, now you don't, as the flames flap and flicker.

Grandma says, "Time for an ogrous, loathsome monster story; a *linani* story. They're the best stories on a dark night like this, aren't they?"

"Yes. Ye-es. Ye-es," say the children a bit shakily.

"There once lived the beautiful Karimirwa and her hunchback sister, Musiguku. Karimirwa is a lovely girl. All the young men for miles around want her for a wife. But Musiguku they never come to see. She has this lump on her back between her shoulders. But Musiguku is a bright girl, very bright. You shouldn't always go by appearances.

Now, Karimirwa and Musiguku live in a house just like this one. And every morning Karimirwa, the beautiful one, takes her hoe and her basket and goes to the fields to work. Musiguku stays behind and does all the jobs around the house, fetching the firewood and water, washing, cleaning and so on.

And every day young men come to the house looking for Karimirwa. Maybe Musiguku's sitting by the fire, cooking and the young man comes up to her and says, 'Milembé, Musiguku! Where's your sister, Karimirwa?'

'Milembé, young man,' says Musiguku, and she looks the young man up and down very carefully. 'Karimirwa's out in the fields working. I'll tell her you came. Come back tomorrow and maybe you'll find her here.'

In the evening when Karimirwa comes back from the fields, Musiguku says to her, 'So-and-So came for you this morning. He's a lazy lad; he wanted me to carry some of my wood to his house.' Or she says, 'So-and-So came for you this morning. He has fingers that thick — like telegraph poles.'

And Karimirwa says, 'No, I don't want him.'

And that happens day after day.

Well, a family of monsters, *linanis*, hear about this lovely girl, Karimirwa. And the young man in this *linani* family decides that he wants to marry Karimirwa.

> "Grandma, what does a *linani* look like?" asks Peter.
>
> "A *linani*, my child, can look like me, or you, or anything," says Grandma. "They can change themselves into anything they want – a dog, an old boot, a donkey, a white man, or even a tree like that one over there, or a bush like this one here."
>
> "Ugh!" We all shiver a bit and shift away from the bush and towards the fire. That bush does look a bit like a *linani*.

Grandma says, "Now, this young *linani* likes the look of Karimirwa. So he changes himself into a handsome young man – really up-to-date he looks. Any mother would be proud to have him as a son-in-law. And he's clever too, this handsome young *linani*. Instead of going to the house, as all the other young men did, he goes to the field, where Karimirwa's working. And he introduces himself.

'*Milembé*, Karimirwa! I'm Sinano. You're working hard, I see.'

'*Milembé*, Sinano!' replies Karimirwa. 'Yes, I'm working hard.' And they have a long conversation, Karimirwa and Sinano. She likes him; in fact, she falls

80

head over heels in love with this *linani* in disguise. And in the evening she brings her boyfriend back home.

Sinano speaks to Karimirwa's parents and asks if he can marry her. Her parents like the look of this up-to-date young man and they say, 'You can marry Karimirwa, if she agrees.'

'Yes, yes, I agree,' says Karimirwa.

And Musiguku's standing there, looking this young man up and down, as she always does.

'My home's a long way away from here,' says Sinano. 'So I hope you don't mind if I don't follow your custom exactly. Instead of bringing you a cow this week and another cow next week and so on, I'll bring you all the cattle as the bride price seven days from now.'

Karimirwa's father looks really pleased at this. 'No, I don't mind getting all the cattle next week,' he says. 'You and the cattle will be most welcome. We'll be ready for you, son-in-law.'

And all the time Musiguku's walking round, looking this young man up and down.

After Sinano's gone, Musiguku says, 'Karimirwa, my duck, don't, please don't marry that man.'

'What! Why on earth not? He's fantastic. He's so handsome, so up-to-date.'

'But can't you see? He's an ogre, a monster, a *linani*, an ogrous *linani*.'

'A *linani*? How do you know that?' asks Karimirwa. 'What a crazy idea! He's the handsomest man I've ever seen.'

Musiguku turns to her father. 'Father, you must stop her marrying that *linani*. Did you look at his finger-nails? They look like claws.'

'Ooo! I hate you. You're no longer my sister, Musiguku. I love Sinano. I love him. I love him. I love him.'

And father says, 'He isn't a *linani*. He's bringing me a lot of cattle next week. You're always turning young men away, Musiguku. And we all know why – you and that lump on your back.'

Musiguku runs from the room sobbing, 'D-d-does it mean that when one's cri-crippled one shouldn't suggest anything? We'll see.'

A week later, as he promised, Sinano, looking very smart, arrives with four other young men, driving a small herd of cattle. As is the custom, Karimirwa's parents welcome the young men. They sit them down and lay plates and plates of food in front of them. Then they leave the room, closing the door behind them because, when people come to the house for marriage, it isn't right to watch them eat.

But Musiguku, the clever girl: she watches them through a crack in the door. And she sees – she nearly falls on the floor in fright – she sees five horrid *linanis*. They've changed back to their real shapes. Five horrid *linanis* – hairy, white-skinned, covered in carbuncles, boils, bunions and bumps.

But Musiguku goes on watching and listening. They eat everything – absolutely everything. Stuff it all into their mouths – wide and round like dustbins and with fangs like lions' teeth.

Yes, everything goes in, even the plates and they're just about to start on the calabashes when Sinano speaks to them in a low, angry *linani* voice.

'You barbarians! You swine! Do you want to shame

me in front of my parents-in-law? That's not the way to behave. Those plates: sick them up! Come on, sick them up again!'

Hur-hur-hurrp!

They sick up the plates onto the table. And Musiguku's watching all this, her knees shivering with fear.

'Come on, you haven't finished yet,' says Sinano. 'You must sick up a bit of the food. Visitors shouldn't eat everything laid before them. It isn't the custom here. Come on, sick it up!'

Hur-hur-hurrp!

They sick up some food onto the plates.

Musiguku watches the *linanis* sicking up all these things and then she runs off to Karimirwa and her parents.

'Please, please don't marry him,' she pleads. 'He's a *linani*. They're all *linanis*.'

'Oh, there you go again,' says her mother. 'We all know why you don't want your sister to marry that handsome young man, you jealous lump.'

'Sister, my dear, dear sister, don't go. They'll eat you. They ate all the food and even the plates,' Musiguku pleads with her sister.

But just then out of the room come the five young men again. Sinano says, 'Thank you for the excellent meal. It's really filled our stomachs. We'll return home now and I'll take my wife, Karimirwa, with me.'

So Sinano, the four young men and Karimirwa set off. As is the custom, all Karimirwa's friends join the group to escort her to her new home. Musiguku goes along with them too. But they turn on her, shouting and waving their arms: 'Clear off! Go on, clear off!

Take your lump somewhere else. You're spoiling our beauty. We'll never find husbands if you come.'

Musiguku says nothing. She just disappears through a gap in the hedge.

"They should listen to her, shouldn't they?" says Grace. "Yes, my child, they should," says Grandma. "But people are very foolish. They think if you have a lump on your back, or a squint in your eye, you have no brains." Grandma pushes another stick into the fire. Flames flare up. And around us in the scary darkness we see shapes; heads, a bush, monsters, a *linani*. Ugh! Grandma grins and her teeth flash white in the firelight. The children shrink away from her. "What's the matter with you?" she says. "Do you think I'm a *linani*?" "Go on, Grandma, what happens next?"

Musiguku's determined to go to the *linanis'* home and save the girls from being eaten. She takes a short cut through the wood and arrives outside the *linanis'* yard before the rest of them. She hides behind a tree and she sees — she sees the horridest *linani* of them all; layers of bubbly fungus and flabbering lumps, bosoms and bums. The *linani's* standing in front of a huge cooking pot, steaming and bubbling over. And this ugly *linani's* singing to itself over and over again as it stirs the pot:

'Their flesh I will chew.
Ho! Ho!
Their blood I will suck.
Ho! Ho!
Their bones I will munch.
Ho! Ho!
But their marrow – bee-oootiful marrow.

mmmMMMMMMX

Karimirwa and her friends are approaching and Musiguku sees the ugly *linani* change into a beautiful girl. When the girls arrive outside the *linanis'* house, Musiguku joins them.

'Let her stay. Let her stay,' says Sinano. 'The more guests there are, the merrier we'll be.' And they all go into the *linanis'* house and sit down.

'Now, what would you like?' asks Sinano very politely.

Quickly Musiguku says, 'We're very thirsty after our journey – so thirsty. We'd like some cool water.'

Sinano and his friends bring them water from the great cooling jar in the corner of the room.

'No, no,' says Musiguku. 'We don't drink river water. In our house we drink lake water.'

Sinano and his friends pick up calabashes and go to the door.

'No, no,' says Musiguku. 'In our house we fetch water in baskets.'

Sinano and his friends pick up baskets and dash off towards the lake.

As soon as they've gone, Musiguku says to Karimirwa and her friends, 'Quick! Let's get away from here. They're all *linanis*. This is a *linani* house. Look at that cooking pot. It's boiling but there's nothing to eat in it. It's for us. It's to cook us in. Come on! Come on!'

And this time they believe her. And they all run, run as fast as they can till they come to a big river. And here they stop because they can't cross it.

Meanwhile Sinano and his friends are on the lake shore, trying to bring water back in their baskets. They draw water, take a step and it runs out. They draw water, take a step and it runs out. Draw more water, take two steps and it runs out. They put mud in the baskets to hold the water, but the mud runs out too.

Grandma puts another stick in the fire and starts poking the flames up. Then she stops. The air shivers with a strange hovering sound as bats flit and jink around our heads. Grandma looks away into the darkness and goes on with the story.

In the end Sinano throws his basket away and says, 'That lump of a girl, Musiguku, she's tricked us. They don't draw water in baskets. Nobody can do that. Quick! Back home before they escape!'

And all the *linanis* come hurtling back home, stampeding, bellowing as they come, jumping the bushes, thundering on the ground:

Gu-boo! Gu-boo! Gu-boo! Gu-boo!
Gu-boo! Gu-boo!

And there's a loud thundering, and the ground begins shaking as the *linanis* come."

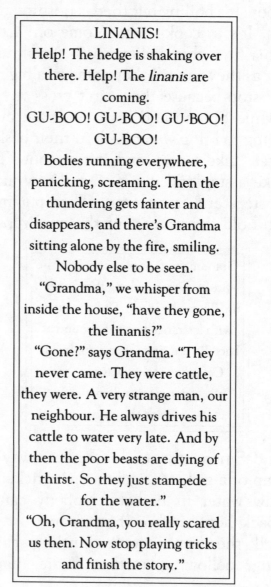

LINANIS!
Help! The hedge is shaking over there. Help! The *linanis* are coming.
GU-BOO! GU-BOO! GU-BOO! GU-BOO!
Bodies running everywhere, panicking, screaming. Then the thundering gets fainter and disappears, and there's Grandma sitting alone by the fire, smiling.
Nobody else to be seen.
"Grandma," we whisper from inside the house, "have they gone, the linanis?"
"Gone?" says Grandma. "They never came. They were cattle, they were. A very strange man, our neighbour. He always drives his cattle to water very late. And by then the poor beasts are dying of thirst. So they just stampede for the water."
"Oh, Grandma, you really scared us then. Now stop playing tricks and finish the story."

"When the *linanis* reach their house, of course they don't find anybody. They are furious, raging with anger.

'That lump, Musiguku,' shouts Sinano. 'I'll eat her first. Come on! Let's go and find them.'

So off they go, all the *linanis*, through the fields, through the woods, looking behind the hedges and everywhere for Karimirwa and the rest, down to the big river. And on the river bank they see a frog, a frog with an enormous belly.

Sinano asks the frog, 'You haven't seen any young girls come this way, have you?'

'Young girls?' says the fat frog. 'Why should young girls come to see a fat, ugly frog like me? But if you can just fling me over to the other side of the river, I may be able to help you.'

Sinano says, 'You've swallowed them. Look at your big belly. They're all in there. Come on, sick them up!'

'Hur-hur-hurrp!' goes the frog and sicks up – a heap of black mud.

'There now, does that satisfy you?' asks the frog. 'Now just fling me across the river, will you, please?'

So Sinano picks up the fat frog and flings it away – away – plop on the other bank of the big river.

The fat frog slowly turns to face the river and says loudly:

'RRREK-KEK-KEK-KEK-KO-AX-KO-AX.
RRREK-KEK-KEK-KEK-KO-AX-KO-AX.'

And the water of the river divides, leaving a dry path across the river from bank to bank. The *linanis* start to run across the river bed. And when they're all in the middle of the river, the frog says again – come on, you must help this time. We want to get rid of those terrible *linanis*, don't we. . . ? . . . The frog says,

'Rrrek-kek-kek-kek-ko-ax-ko-ax.
Rrrek-kek-kek-kek-ko-ax-ko-ax.'

Louder than that. Come on, much louder. Wash the *linanis* away.

'RRREK–KEK–KEK–KEK–KO–AX–KO–AX.'

That's right. And the river starts flowing again, and washes all those *linanis* away down the river. And good riddance.

Then, slowly, very slowly, because he's so fat and heavy, the frog creeps to the village where Musiguku and the girls live. The frog goes into the garden of the first house and sits down.

'Ugh!' they say. 'Ugh! A frog! Bring a stick and push it out.' So they bring a stick and push the frog out.

The frog goes to the next house and the same thing happens again. And the next, and the next, and so on till he reaches the home of Karimirwa and Musiguku. In the yard there's an old woman sitting by the fire with Karimirwa's younger brothers and sisters. The huge frog goes up to them and sits beside them.

'Ugh! Ugh!' scream the children. 'A frog! Take it away!'

'No, no,' says the old woman. 'Leave it alone. It's tired; it's come a long way.'

'Take it away! Is a frog worth our two dead sisters?'

The old woman pays no attention. She brings some ointment from her house and rubs it gently all over the frog. 'There now,' she says. 'Is that better?'

'Rrrelaaax! Rrrelaaax! Rrrelaaax!' croaks the frog.

'Well then,' says the old woman, 'now let's see what's in your belly. Come on! One – two – three.'

Hur-hur-hurrp!

And out come Musiguku, Karimirwa and all their friends. Safe and sound. Singing and dancing for joy, praising Musiguku for her courage:

> 'Happy and
> healthy and
> singing and
> dancing and
> *free as the wind are we*
> *free as the wind are we*
> *free as the wind are we.*
> Happy and . . .' "

91

· 7 ·

There's One Day for the Victim

"Once upon a time . . . Come on you two. Where are you? Once upon a time; once upon a time! Don't you want a story tonight?"

"Coming, Grandad," says a voice from inside the house. "We've nearly finished clearing away the supper." Sounds of metal on metal and plate on plate from within the house.

A few minutes later Toro and her little brother, Kunle, come out into the courtyard, from the world of work and washing to the world of dreams and stories. In the moonlight the courtyard is made of silver tinfoil and the air is silver seethrough. At the far end of the courtyard the house-high wall stands in dark shadow. From near the bottom of the shadow two eyes blink, white on black, and a set of teeth flash, wide and white. Sticking out of the shadow towards us into the silver moonlight is a pair of slippered feet.

"Over here," says Grandad. "Come and sit here." A hand comes out of the shadow and pats the silver earth. Toro and Kunle sit in the moonlight by Grandad, while overhead voices float over the high wall, the voices of people in the street outside and the sounds of feet passing this way and that in the town.

"Which story are you going to tell us tonight, Grandad?" asks Toro.

"I'll tell you how the tough guys got a taste of their own medicine. Bullies are at work every day, but once in a while a day comes when they suffer as they deserve.

"Once upon a time there was a family that lived with Hunger. Their yesterdays began with hunger pains; their todays bring only despair and their tomorrows will end with death . . .

No, my children. No! This is no matter you should laugh at. When hunger enters the house by the door, then happiness flies out through the windows and the family lives with sadness and suffering.

Your parents have brought you food and shelter. But every night I pray to God that you, my children, when you are parents, may also bring food and shelter to your children. Hunger: when once it sinks its teeth into your life, Hunger is king.

Now this unfortunate family lived with Hunger, day in, day out. And Death: Death was slowly sharpening his pencil to write in his diary the day when he would meet them. No crops grew in their fields. They had no money to buy food and the pains of starvation bit sharper and sharper. As the weeks passed, the shine faded from their faces and their plumpness melted like mist. Their bodies were no more than skin draped over bones, like grey canvas on a market stall. The large heads of the children lolled on their shoulders, and in front their bellies blew out like sails on a boat. And everywhere, all the time, the pains of Hunger bit and bit and bit. Hunger is terrible, my children.

> "Grandad, I didn't have any
> breakfast this morning because I
> slept too long," says Kunle. "And
> then I felt sort of empty inside. Is
> that hunger?"
> Grandad says, "Well, my child,
> that's just going without *one* meal.
> Imagine going without *all* meals
> tomorrow, the day after and as far
> into the days as you can think.
> That's hunger."
> "But it hurts."
> "Yes, it hurts. And it goes on
> hurting, and on and on. And if you
> don't find food, death is a release
> from the hurting."

Now the oldest child in this family, a boy, a teenager, almost a man, heard Death slowly sharpening his pencil:

kss – kss – kss – kss – kss – kss – kss

and he decided he would go and look for Life. 'If I'm going to die,' he said to himself, 'it would be better for me to die on my feet than in my bed.'

So he said goodbye to his parents and his brothers and sisters and walked to the nearest town.

The first town he came to was bustling with activity. Business was booming and the people had never seen Hunger. They looked at the young man and they laughed. They laughed and gave him no work.

'You! Work?' they said. 'What kind of worker are you? What are you good for? Bone bag, you can hardly lift your own head; how can you lift a sack of corn? Kitten-floppy, you can hardly stick a knife in a potato; how can you stick a spade in the ground? Skeleton, why do you trouble us with your bones? You spoil the view. Get out of our town. On your way. Go on!' They didn't give him anything to eat. In that town Hunger was not recognized, and the people were hard-faced, busy and pitiless.

So the young man walked on to the next town and to the next and on to the next. But in every town it was the same. If he asked for food, they told him to work. If he asked for work, they gave him abuse. If he asked them for charity in the name of God and their ancestors, they told him to ask his own God and his own ancestors. They were indeed hard people. Hunger was his companion; Death was his destination.

The young man continued on his journey in search of Life and he walked on to the next town.

And it so happened that, when the young man reached this town, his calabash of misfortunes was empty. It was in this town that the young man escaped from Hunger; it was in this town that Death stopped sharpening a pencil for him. The young man walked out of Death and into Life.

And this was how it happened.

As the young man entered the town, the town crier was walking through the streets, ringing his bell and announcing to the citizens: 'Oyez! Oyez! Oyez! To all citizens of this town and to all friends and visitors. The king, his majesty the Oba, sends you his greetings and

hopes you are all in good health as he is himself. But
this day the Oba has lost a ring of great value, a ring
made of gold. The ring is carved in the bodies of three
snakes; the snake in the middle is the largest and in its
mouth it holds a diamond. To the left and right are two
smaller snakes, each with a red ruby in its mouth. His
majesty the Oba makes this solemn promise: he will
richly reward the person, man, woman, or child, who
brings this ring back to him. Oyez! Oyez! Oyez!'

As the young man was trudging through the town,
his head heavy and weighed down flat with his shoulders, his eyes caught sight of the ring. Yes, the ring, the
Oba's ring, made of gold and carved with three snakes
holding two red rubies and the diamond, flashing in
the dust of the street.

This was Life; this ring shining in the dust. It was

food. It was strength. It was happiness. The young man's heart jumped as he picked the ring up. His steps were light, and he held himself straight as he turned towards the Oba's palace. In his hand he held the end of Hunger. He held Life.

Now the Oba was a man of great wealth. He lived with his wives in a large palace. The palace was surrounded by fields that stretched to the horizon. The fields were full of the Oba's wealth, full of his crops and his granaries, full of his fat-tailed sheep, his goats and his cattle. Round all this was a wall, a battlement, higher than a house. And in this wall was one gate, solid wood with iron studs the size of manhole covers. In front of the gate stood the gatekeeper.

When I tell you this gatekeeper was tall, it's a tree you must think of. When I tell you this gatekeeper was huge, it's a gorilla you must think of. When I tell you this gatekeeper was strong, it's a weightlifter you must think of. From the ends of his forearms his fists burst like cabbage heads, and his biceps rose like the bulge on a jumbo jet. A mountain of muscle was this man. A brainless brute of unspeakable violence was the gatekeeper. And it was to this monster that the young man came whose calabash of misfortunes was empty.

'Excuse me, I'd like to see the Oba, please.'

The gatekeeper grinned down at the young man. With a forefinger he picked a scab from his cheek and he said:

'I am Big Bonecrusher, Champion of Champions. Hah! Today I will send you to your grave; with my heel I can press you flat as a rat on tarmac. Today I will close your mouth for good; with my hand I can fling you in orbit. Today I will add *you* to my score; with my head I can smash you in splinters. Have you not heard? I am Big Bonecrusher and I let no one pass this gate.'

Fear filled the young man. He shook. He shivered. He froze with fright. Terror glued his bones together.

But strong as this fear was, the young man's hunger was stronger. Just as he had walked on when he was frightened of death from hunger, so he spoke on now he was frightened of death from this gatekeeper. 'But you must let me pass. I've found the Oba's ring.' And he opened his hand to show the ring to the gatekeeper.

The gatekeeper said, 'Didn't you hear me? I – am – Big – Bonecrusher, the Champion of all Champions. Have you no brains in your skull? I – AM – BIG – BONECRUSHER. I – AM – THE – GREATEST. I let no one, I repeat, no one pass this gate till he gives me a gift. What gift can you give ME, the Champion of all Champions? Give me the ring, I say. What use is the ring to you when I won't let you pass? Hah! Today I will snuff out your life; with my thumb I can squash you like a redcurrant. You must give the ring to me, Big Bonecrusher, the Champion of Champions.'

The young man said, 'Let me pass and I promise I'll give you half the reward the Oba gives me.'

Amazement spread over the gatekeeper's face and in his heart greed grew like mould. I tell you his mind writhed with hankering like a worm cut in half. The gatekeeper grinned down at the young man. He flexed his cabbage-head fists, cracked his finger bones and said, 'If I don't get my share, I'll peel your skin strip by strip from head to foot like a banana. I'll mash you to baby food. I'll knead you to pink Plasticine for my children.' And he opened wide the great gate. The young man passed through and behind him the gate thumped shut.

He walked along the driveway to the palace. In this place there was peace and prosperity. In the Oba's land there had never been hunger or suffering. To the left were fields of sorghum and maize, to the right were pastures where cattle were grazing. In front was the palace, an immense building with towers at the four corners and a wall that had no windows and just one door in the middle. The young man knocked.

The door opened and there stood a little black shape, the doorkeeper, a man about as small as the young man himself. An ordinary, harmless man he looked. The young man's fear melted; his anxiety faded like smoke in the air. And he smiled.

'Wipe that smirk off your face, boy!' said the doorkeeper. With one hand he grabbed the young man round his neck and held him face to face. With his tongue the doorkeeper licked the tip of the young man's nose and said, 'Scum! My name is Black Scut and I don't care a tea leaf who you are.' And dropped him like a wet blanket on the ground.

Alarm crawled over the back of the young man's scalp like a crab. When he looked up at the doorkeeper, fear flickered in snakes' tongues down his spine and in his chest terror stopped his breath.

The doorkeeper was dressed all in black. Black were his boots. Black was his robe from the ground to his shoulders. Black were the bracelets he wore round his wrists. Black were the frames of his sunglasses and black was his cap. But his lips were red flesh, gashed by a butcher's knife. And instead of eyes the lenses of his glasses were deep, blue holes that sucked you, pulled you, dragged you down into their depths to drown.

Spellbound the young man gazed into the holes. Hypnotized he stared into the death traps:

kss − kss − kss − kss − kss − kss − kss − kss − kss.

But it wasn't death the young man wanted. Life was all that belonged to him and it was life he was struggling to keep. He said to the doorkeeper, 'Excuse me, I'd like to see the Oba, please.'

The face moved. The red flesh split and words crept out. They treacled over the young man as over a crumb:

'Cud in cow's mouth!
Clod!
Waif!
Pinhole blast from mouse bum!
Take a look at yourself. What are you?
You ribcage wonder! You swellbelly!
Who are you?
Where do you come from? Where do you think you are going?

Greater things than you have failed to pass my door. Their finger bones were a snack for my cat; their leg bones a dinner for my dog. And their skulls I use as flower pots.

You soft moth!
Can you understand it's death you're breathing now?'

Like a dead cat dragged from a hole the young man heaved himself up off the ground and replied, 'I have lived with death for many days. In my belly he's made his work-place. My hunger pains are his wages. The

100

money I have left to pay him wastes away by the hour. The death of the hungry lasts longer than the way to the stars. The death of the hungry hurts more than the loss of a loved one. The death of the hungry is more frightening than murder. But death from a mere doorkeeper takes no longer than a clock tick. You must let me pass. I have found the Oba's ring.' He opened his hand to show the doorkeeper the ring.

The doorkeeper replied,

'You small, small millet seed thing!

You frog's spawn fleck!

Is that how you speak to me, Black Scut? Are those the words you pour in my ears? Is that the speech you lay at my feet? Then, prepare yourself. The death I'll give you will be a thousand times more agonizing than death from hunger. Prepare yourself, you rag doll!

Your screams will shrink the moon.'

The young man said, 'If you let me pass, I'll give you half the reward the Oba gives me.'

'Only half? If I don't take the whole of the reward the Oba gives you and use your skin as a floor cloth, then my name is no longer Black Scut and you may spit in my face. Pass, maggot!'

The doorkeeper swung the door open and the young man stepped from the heat of the overhead sun into the shade of the palace.

The rooms of the palace were many; they were cool; they were perfumed and they whispered with the sound of water plashing in a fishpool in the centre of the courtyard. Round the pool, banana trees rose and their great leaves fanned overhead like the moving pillars of a green cathedral. And on the surface of the water, lilies spread their round faces, purple and pink.

Past the pool the young man trudged, a grey ghost carrying death in his stomach and life in his hand. When he came to the room where the Oba was, he threw himself flat on the floor in front of him and said, 'Kabiyesi! I greet your majesty.'

Shocked was the Oba when he saw the young man. Sorrow flowed through his body to the corners of his eyes. Such suffering in his kingdom the Oba had never seen; such hunger he had never guessed. Truly the young man was a sight to make you weep.

The Oba said, 'Rise and tell me how it has happened that one of my citizens walks in my kingdom as a corpse walks in the kingdom of death.'

The young man replied, 'First, your majesty, I must tell you that I bring you your ring.' And he showed the ring to the Oba.

Delight like cream between slices of orange curled round the sorrow in the Oba's heart. He said, 'Food, of course, I'll provide for your stomach. Bring him food! Bring him food! But what shall be your reward for finding my ring? Choose and I'll give.'

'The reward I want is one hundred strokes of the cane.'

In the Oba's heart surprise clashed with delight. Amazement tangled with sorrow and his tongue could find no words.

When his heart was calm he said, 'One hundred strokes of the cane! But it isn't punishment I want to give you, it's a reward. When you have done no wrong, why is it punishment you want?'

And the young man told the Oba what had happened to him at the gate and the door. The Oba's body shook with amusement; his eyes danced. He could hold back his smiles no longer and laughter burst from the Oba as the wind billows the curtains open. 'Eat, while I speak to those two servants of mine, the gatekeeper and the doorkeeper.'

When the two servants arrived, they stretched themselves flat on the floor in front of the Oba and said, 'Kabiyesi! We greet your majesty.'

'Stay on your faces. Is it true,' the Oba asked the gatekeeper, 'that this young man has promised you half his reward?'

'Yes, Kabiyesi,' replied the mountainous gatekeeper on his face on the floor.

'And is it true,' the Oba asked the doorkeeper, 'that this young man has also promised YOU half his reward?'

'Yes, Kabiyesi,' replied the doorkeeper, dressed all in black, and his face on the floor.

The Oba laughed and said, 'Any day does for the tough guy but there's one day – one day that's reserved for the victim. Stay on your faces and prepare to receive your reward. The reward the young man has asked for is one hundred strokes of the cane. Call my wrestler to punish these men.'

After the two servants had received fifty strokes of the cane each, the Oba said to the young man, 'Your reward for finding my ring you have now received, but your reward for catching my two shameless servants is still to be given you.'

For a week the young man ate well in the palace and, when he returned to his family, a long line of the Oba's

servants followed him, each servant carrying gifts on his head.

For the family their hunger was finished and life had begun."

"There," says Grandad, "and that's how the young man escaped death from hunger."

"Ugh!" exclaims Toro, shivering. "I never want to be hungry like that. Ugh!"

"No," says Grandad, "but it happens and I pray God it never happens while you're alive."

The moon has moved round and Grandad is now sitting in the moonlight, looking like a white man in his white gown and patterned hat. There are no insects to be heard but all the dogs in town, near and far, are howling as they often do when the moon is bright.

· 8 ·

Hare and the White Man

"Supper's ready!" That's Teko calling her cousins, Modisé and his younger sister, Kebonye. Modisé's been playing with his wire lorry. It's his latest model and he's been driving it all over the place, testing it, a noisy thing, tinkling along like a box of tin bells. A wheel fell off and he had to fit the spare wheel. He's now using plastic lids from coffee jars as wheels, instead of old bean tins, because it's easier to make a wheel from a lid than by cutting bean tins in half.

Kebonye's been playing Tin Touch with several other bigger children. She's good because she's small and quick, and it's difficult to hit her with the ball.

Teko's older than her cousins, so she's been doing a big girl's job of helping the mother of Modisé and Kebonye prepare the supper. They have a very special guest tonight, Aunt Gladys, Teko's mother, on a rare visit from Johannesburg. A few years ago when Kebonye was very small, she once inspected all the donkeys in the neighbouroود after a visit from Aunt Gladys to see if they still had their hind legs because her mother had said, "Talk the hind leg off a donkey, your Aunt Gladys would."

Modisé and Kebonye arrive, singing their supper

106

song over and over again:

> "Fire, fire, lick the pot,
> make its sides black and hot.
> Fire, fire, cook the food.
> Mm! Mm! Tasting good."

They greet their aunt, *"Dumela mma!"* shake hands with her, sit down and start eating.

They're all sitting on orange boxes in their kitchen – a stick shelter with no roof, built onto the end wall of their house. The shelter protects the fire from the dusty winds that blow across the flat plain stretching to the horizon in all directions. A large pot, half full of porridge, is sitting on three stones in the middle of the kitchen. The porridge is still bubbling slightly although the fire underneath it is out. No point in wasting wood when you have to bring it all yourself on your head for miles.

It's just about sunset and it's getting dark. There's a crescent moon in the sky and the insects are beginning their night music. There are several other houses nearby, all with old tyres, great boulders and blocks on their flat roofs to stop the roofs blowing off when the wind's strong.

Not far away, the windpump's squeaking round, pumping water up from underground. In the distance is a clump of trees, some bushes and the water sprinklers that never stop watering the lawns and flowers around the big house where the white farmer and his family live. The children's mother works for the farmer. Their father they hardly ever see because he's a miner in a gold mine in Johannesburg.

When they've finished eating, it's dark except for a faint light from the moon, a luminous nail-clipping hanging up there high above a line of small yellow rectangles — the windows of the farmhouse lit with electric light.

"Do you know the story of Hare and the white man?" asks Aunt Gladys.

"No."

In fact, they do. The children know it very well. But they haven't heard Aunt tell the story. She's sure to tell it in a different way.

"Well, you know what sort of animal a hare is, don't you?" says Aunt.

"Yes, clever and very tricky," says Modisé.

"And what do you know about white people?"

"They're clever too," says Kebonye.

"Hm! Some are, some ain't," says Aunt. "Some are suckers, some ain't. Some lord it over you, some don't. Mind you, they say there's one born every day as you'll see in this story.

It is said that one day Hare was in the bush, cooking porridge all on his own-io. Don't ask me why he was cooking porridge in the bush. There's plenty of things in the world these days we don't know the answers to, I can tell you. But there he was, cooking porridge in the bush. What with firewood being all over the place, he had a big fire going and the large pot was plopping away like mad. Hare was just sitting there, watching this pot when he noticed, far away in the distance, a white man on a horse coming in his direction.

108

Talk about greased lightning, that hare was faster, believe me. He must have had a thing about white men: a persecution complex, perhaps, and with good reason, I can tell you. In ten seconds flat Hare had put the fire out, chucked the burning branches and the ash all over the place, kicked sand over everything and put fresh sand under the pot. No matter how closely you looked, you'd 've swore blind there hadn't been no fire there. Mind you, the blooming pot was still on its three stones, the porridge still plopping away like mad. There wasn't nothing Hare could do about that. And he certainly wasn't going to chuck good food away into the bargain.

Anyway, up rode the white man and there was Hare, just sitting beside this plopping pot, looking all innocent as if butter wouldn't melt in his mouth. Hare says, '*Dumela, rra!*'

'How do you do that?' says the white man. He wasn't looking at Hare; he was looking at the plopping pot.

'Do what?'

'That. Make the pot cook by itself without a fire,' says the white man.

'Oh, that,' says Hare. 'That. It's a self-cooker.'

'A self-cooker,' says the white man. 'But how does it work? I don't see any gas or electricity.'

'Oh, I just say to it, "*Pitsa, apaya motogo*",' says Hare.

> The children laugh. Modisé looks at the pot standing in the middle and says, "*Pitsa, apaya motogo.*"
> But nothing happens.
> Modisé says to his mother,

> "Why don't we have a self-cooker?
> We needn't go for wood then."
> Mother laughs and says, "Well,
> I'm not a hare.
> I'm just a human being."
> "Anyway," says Aunt, going on
> with the story, "*Pitsa, apaya
> motogo.*"

'And what does that mean when it's at home?' says the white man.

'It means "Pot, cook porridge",' says Hare.

'How much will you sell it for?' says the white man.

'Five hundred rand,' says Hare, holding his hand out.

'Three hundred.'

'Four hundred.'

'Done,' says the white man. He fished four hundred rand out of his pocket, took the pot and tipped the porridge out as if it was something the cat brought in. Then he tied the pot to his saddle and off he rode.

Well, of course, it was no surprise when the white man got home and tried out his new self-cooker – it didn't work, did it? Perhaps he couldn't remember what to say to it; or he couldn't pronounce our language properly. I don't know. Anyway, cook by itself – that was what that pot could not or would not do.

Now you don't need me to tell you that nobody likes to be had for a sucker, do they? Livid that white man was, believe me. Not only livid, but he felt himself to be an object of ridicule. What with him being a white

man and Hare being only a hare, he felt Hare had taken him for a ride. He picked up the pot and off he stormed to the *kgotla,* the parliament for hares, ready for a battle royal.

When the white man arrived, the hares were already having a meeting in the *kgotla* – the chief hare sitting in front with his advisers. Up stalks the white man and bangs the pot down on the table, fit to drive it into the ground.

'*Dumela rra!*' says the chief.

'I bought this here pot from one of your . . .'

'*Dumela rra!*' says the chief again, a bit louder.

'*Dumela ra,*' says the white man, in his best Setswana.

'Welcome to our *kgotla,* white man. What's your business?'

'I bought this pot from one of your hares,' says the white man. 'And he lied to me that it was a self-cooking pot. But it ain't. It's just an ordinary pot.'

The chief says, 'That is a serious charge. I don't like it when one of my hares is accused of cheating somebody. We will deal with your case now. If you can identify the hare that sold you the pot, I will call him up here and we will listen to your complaint.'

The white man looked at the hares sitting in front of him – all of three hundred there were, without exaggerating. 'That one,' he says. 'No, that one . . . no! Well . . . erm! I don't know. You hares all look alike. Peas in a pod, the lot of you'.

'Try again,' says the chief. 'We are all different.'

But it was no good. From the point of view of identifying hares, that white man was a dead loss, I can tell you. He couldn't make out which hare cheated him.

The chief says, 'Since you cannot identify the hare that sold you the pot, I must punish you. It is a serious matter to waste the time of the *kgotla*. It is an even more serious matter to make an accusation you cannot prove. I fine you five hundred rand.'

So, the white man had to pay five hundred rand to the *kgotla*, the parliament for hares.

As I said, he was livid to start with, but that was nothing compared to what he was now, believe me. He was livid fit to bust, AND break up the world into the bargain. Talk about a white man, this one was purple. And the funny thing was, he didn't even take the pot with him when he left."

"But why couldn't the white man recognize the hare that cheated him?" asks Kebonye.

"Well," says Aunt, "there ain't many white people in this area, so you know them all. But come back with me to Johannesburg next week and see the crowds of white people there. You've got to admit you'll be as useless at identifying them as the man in the story was."

Perhaps you'd like to know something about the game of Tin Touch and about wire lorries.

TIN TOUCH. This game is often played by children in some parts of Africa. It can be played by children of different ages — the small ones are as useful as the big ones.

You need — two teams of about eight each.

– about six tins of different sizes that will fit on top of each other to build a tower.

– two parallel lines about 8-10 metres apart.

– a soft ball.

One team must remain between the lines and try to build up the tower of tins. When the tower is built, the builder must beat the ground three times with one hand on each side of the tower to make sure the tower can really stand by itself, then knock the tower down. The team builds the tower again. The other team stands outside the lines and tries to hit the builders or the tower with the ball. Any builder who is hit is out. The throwers can throw only from outside the lines, though they may come inside the lines to pick the ball up. The winner is the team which builds the tower most often before all members of the team are out.

WIRE LORRIES. Many boys in Africa spend a lot of their spare time making and driving wire lorries. It is a highly skilled job.

You need — lots of wire of different sorts: chicken wire, fence wire, dynamo wire.

– some small bean tins, or lids of jars.

– any bits of coloured plastic for windscreens, head-lights, winkers, etc.

– other bits of tin.

Those are the easy things you need. You also need lots of time, lots of patience, and endless skill.

All lorries can be steered and the best ones can carry things.

· 9 ·

Hare and his Friends

Rebecca and Daniel are excited. Their elder brother, Edward, is back from boarding school today and that means a story tonight. A story right now, in fact.

The hurricane lamp's already alight and standing on the table. The room's full of giant, moving shadows as they walk around, fastening the windows tight. The wind's increasing and there's going to be a tremendous thunderstorm soon. Away in the west the sky's flickering with lightning and in the blue-white light you can see towering thunderclouds, boiling and twisting high overhead.

Rrrrrrmmmm!

There's the first roll of thunder in the distance. The storm'll be here soon.

Grandma's gone to bed early – not because of the storm. She's always angry when Edward tells a story. "Hmph!" she grumbles. "Things go from bad to worse. When I was your age, children never told stories; they always listened. You soon won't need grandmas at all. I might as well bury myself right now."

"Sh!" says Edward, a bit shocked. "You shouldn't say things like that. Of course we need you. From who else

116

can we hear the stories that we study in school? But nowadays we learn not just your stories, but stories from all over Africa."

But Grandma still went to bed. "Perhaps it's just as well she's gone," says Edward. "I'm going to tell you a funny story about Sungura, the hare. It's from the Luo people. When Grandma was our age, our people and the Luo were enemies. Grandma would certainly not be pleased that I'm telling you one of their stories. But it's different today and we must move with the times."

The wind's really strong now, rattling the doors and windows. There's so much lightning out there you could still see if you put the lamp out. The thunder's still rather faint and far away. But leaves and twigs, blown from the trees nearby, are pattering on the corrugated metal roof and making it difficult to hear. So, Edward, Rebecca and Daniel and their three friends huddle closely round the table, their faces lit by the glow from the hurricane lamp. And Edward begins:

"There was a time when Sungura tried to make friends with the other animals. One day he went round to Eagle's house.

'Hodi!' said Sungura at the door.

'Karibu!' replied Eagle and Sungura went in.

And they passed the morning chatting pleasantly of this and that, and their friendship grew. But when lunch time came, Sungura was a bit upset to see that Eagle was preparing only bread and vegetables to eat, no meat as was the custom when visitors came.

Well, by now Eagle and Sungura were such good friends that they were talking about anything – even

117

each others' wives and the food they cooked. So Sungura said, 'Haven't you forgotten something, Eagle, my friend? This bread's not enough to fill a man's stomach.'

'Stay cool, man. Stay cool,' said Eagle. 'Everything's under control.' And he continued sitting there, chatting happily with Sungura, who was getting hungrier and hungrier at the thought of no meat for lunch.

At last Eagle rose from his chair and flew off to the nearest village, where there were many chickens pecking around the village square. Eagle dived down:

Eeeeeeee-ow Pow!

He hooked himself a fine, fat chicken. He brought it back in his claws, still squawking loudly, and landed in front of Sungura.

Sungura wasn't at all impressed by this – or at least he pretended he wasn't. He liked to pretend he knew everything – you know the sort of person I mean . . .? . . . He'd done everything and seen everything. A bit of a bore Sungura was; altogether too big for his boots.

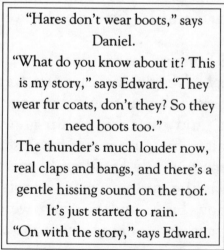

"Hares don't wear boots," says
Daniel.
"What do you know about it? This is my story," says Edward. "They wear fur coats, don't they? So they need boots too."
The thunder's much louder now, real claps and bangs, and there's a gentle hissing sound on the roof.
It's just started to rain.
"On with the story," says Edward.

Too big for his boots, Sungura was. He just sat there, looking at the chicken Eagle had brought back. 'Not bad,' said Sungura, examining his nails. 'Do that any time we need chicken round my place – any time. Duck too!'

Now a few days later, as was the custom, Eagle called at Sungura's house.

'*Hodi!*' said Eagle at the door.

'*Karibu!*' replied Sungura and Eagle went in. And they sat there chatting pleasantly all morning, just as before.

When lunch time came, Eagle was a bit surprised to see that there was no meat, only bread and greens to eat.

'Sungura, my friend,' said Eagle, 'is that all you have for us to eat – bread and greens?'

'Stay cool, man. Stay cool,' said Sungura. 'Don't get your feathers in a twist. Everything's under control.' And Sungura hared off to the nearest village to catch a chicken.

There were plenty of chickens there, doing what chickens always do. Sungura raced around, scattering chickens in all directions, but the chickens were much too quick for him, and they could fly. The farmer happened to be there picking maize seed from the cobs. He pelted Sungura with maize cobs and drove him away.

Sungura returned home, dripping with sweat but with no chicken. Eagle eyed him up and down and asked – as if he didn't know the answer already, 'What's the matter, my friend? What have you been running around for?'

Sungura didn't answer but walked up and down in front of Eagle, mumbling to himself, 'Hmph! Why does the whole world have to gang up on me just when I have my best friend to lunch? Go to catch a chicken like I always do and they almost kill me with maize cobs. Hrrmph! Eagle, my good friend, would you mind catching a chicken for me?'

So Eagle flew off to the village and dived down:

Eeeeeeeee-ow Pow!

He hooked another fine, fat chicken and came back to Sungura with it.

That was the end of that friendship. Sungura was highly embarrassed that Eagle had had to go and catch a chicken for him. 'Eagle's so shameless,' said Sungura to himself. 'Fancy making me embarrassed like that. Friends like that aren't the sort of friends I need.' Sungura turned pink all over with shame.

> "Hares don't go pink," says Daniel.
> "Listen, my little pip-squeak," says
> Edward, "elephants are much
> bigger and they go pink. So why
> not hares? This is my story and if
> you keep on interrupting you'll get
> what you deserve."
> The rain's beating in loud gusts on
> the roof and it's creeping under the
> door. So Rebecca puts a towel
> there to keep the water out. The
> storm's very near now and the
> children put their faces close round
> the lamp so that they can hear
> Edward.

The next friend Sungura called on was Fat Beetle.

'Hodi!' said Sungura at the door.

'Karibu!' said Fat Beetle and Sungura walked in.

They sat around all morning talking and by lunch time their friendship had grown very close. But Sungura was worried to see they were preparing to cook the food for lunch and there wasn't any cooking oil.

Eventually Sungura could contain himself no longer and he blurted out, 'Oil! Oil! You need oil, my friend. The food'll get burnt.'

'Don't worry,' said Fat Beetle. 'Everything's under control. We always have oil in this house.' Then Fat Beetle said to his daughter: 'Child, just bring me that bowl that's warming by the fire, will you?'

Fat Beetle's daughter brought the hot bowl from the fire and Fat Beetle pressed it to his tummy. Hot fat oozed out of Fat Beetle's skin and soon the bowl was full of oil for cooking.

Sungura watched this without turning a hair. He didn't show how impressed he was. Not a bit of it. He just sat there smoothing his whiskers and said, 'Ah, yes, of course. We do that every day at my place. I didn't know you could do it too.'

A few days later, as was the custom, Fat Beetle turned up at Sungura's house.

'Hodi!'

'Karibu!' and Fat Beetle entered Sungura's house. Sungura put a bowl on the fire and then the two friends sat there all morning drinking and talking.

When the time came to cook the food for lunch, Sungura fished the bowl off the fire with a stick and sat on it.

WOY!

And leapt high up in the air. He came back down again, yelling with pain and his bottom on fire. He had to scrape his bottom on the ground for several minutes before it stopped smoking."

"So now they can have roast hare for lunch," says Daniel.

"Now listen here, bright spark," says Edward. "Who's telling this story, you or me?"

"I am," says Daniel, all perky.

fffflashB*NGGGGgggGGGGgggg

"Fwogh!" exclaims Edward. "That was a close one. Where's Daniel? Daniel? Daniel, you can come out now."

Daniel's under the table.

And now there's a tremendous roar on the roof. It's hailing – hailstones as big as thumbnails and you can't hear anything else. So they go to the window and look out. It's all white out there. "This is what it looks like in England in winter," says Edward.

"How do you know?" asks Rebecca.

"I've read about it in books. And it's so cold the water becomes as hard as stone and you can walk on it."

"Oh, yes," says Daniel, cleaning his fingernails. "I do that every day here." When the hailstorm's over Edward goes on with the story.

"So that was the end of that friendship.

Now, the next house Sungura visited belonged to Kurroo, the dove.

'Hodi!'

'Karibu!' and Sungura walked into Kurroo's house. It

123

was a beautiful sunny day and Kurroo had laid out many different kinds of grain on drying mats to dry in the sun. Lunch at Kurroo's went without a hitch. Nothing unusual happened at all. In the afternoon Sungura and Kurroo went outside to talk in the fresh air, and it seemed as if Sungura really was going to find a friend at last.

Towards evening, however, enormous stormclouds came up fast. It was obviously going to rain very heavily and that would ruin Kurroo's grain. And there was so much of it, and so many different sorts, lying all over the yard, drying. But Kurroo just sat on, chatting with Sungura, who was getting more and more fidgety.

In the end, after the wind-before-the-rain had passed and you could see the rain approaching fast, Sungura could contain himself no longer. 'Kurroo, my dear friend,' he said, 'your grain. It'll get spoilt. It'll take a dozen people to carry it all in before it rains.'

'Don't worry!' said Kurroo. 'Everything'll be all right. We're used to this here.' And the dove sat on a bit longer talking to Sungura, who was no longer listening but watching the approaching rainstorm in horror.

Then, just before it started to rain, Kurroo stood up and sang her dove's song:

> 'Now move to the store in Kurroo's room.
> Now move to the pot in Kurroo's room.
> Now move to the box in Kurroo's room.
> Now move to the sack in Kurroo's room.
> Now move to the jar in Kurroo's room.'

124

And sure enough, each type of grain trickled off to its proper storing place – the maize to the store, the wheat to the pot, the sorghum to the box and so on. And last of all, Kurroo and Sungura moved inside with their chairs to shelter from the rain. Not a grain got wet.

And Sungura? Well, you know by now how he behaved, don't you? He just sat there straightening the fur that had got a bit ruffled when he was fidgeting about, and he said, 'Oh, yes, of course! Of course; child's play! I do that when it rains too.'

When he arrived home, Sungura prepared for Kurroo's return visit. He raced round all his neighbours, begging a dozen different types of grain. And he had it out all over the place, drying in the sunshine when Kurroo came a few days later.

A lovely sunny day, it was. But Sungura was praying for rain. My, how he prayed; he even asked Donkey to pray for rain too! Hare's eyes were bulging with prayer, the way hares' eyes do.

At last, his prayers were granted. Clouds appeared over the horizon, huge swelling balloons of white cotton drifting overhead on black frying-pan bottoms. It was obviously going to rain – and rain very heavily.

'Better start bringing your grain in, my friend,' said Kurroo, looking at the clouds.

'Relax! Relax!' said Sungura. 'All in good time. Let's have another drink, shall we?' So they had another drink.

Sungura waited till the wind had passed and you could see the rain coming across the fields towards them. Then he stood up and sang in his toneless hare's voice:

'Now move to the stew pot in Sungura's room.
Now move to the store in Sungura's kitchen.
Now hurry to the tea chest in Sungura's room.
Go on, be off to Sungura's pantry.'

Nothing moved. The rain splashed down like water in
the sink; the grain was soaked in a minute and
completely spoilt. Sungura was highly embarrassed and
turned to Kurroo: 'Kurroo, my friend, can you sing your
song to bring my grain in?'

Kurroo sang but it wasn't any good. The grain was
too wet to move now. Kurroo was really annoyed at
this stupid hare. When it stopped raining, she left and
that was the end of that friendship.

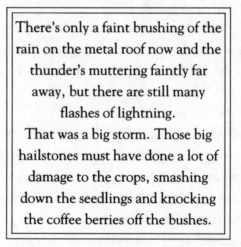

There's only a faint brushing of the
rain on the metal roof now and the
thunder's muttering faintly far
away, but there are still many
flashes of lightning.
That was a big storm. Those big
hailstones must have done a lot of
damage to the crops, smashing
down the seedlings and knocking
the coffee berries off the bushes.

You'd think Sungura would have learnt something by
now, wouldn't you? After all, he's supposed to be the
cleverest of all the animals. But he hadn't learnt a
thing about friendship. He was still trying to be the
know-all. So he tried once more.

This time he went to Crocodile's house. Crocodile

lived on an island in the middle of the river and he carried Sungura over on his back to his house on the island.

'*Hodi!*'

'*Karibu!*' said Mrs Crocodile and Sungura went in.

Crocodile was having a party that night and there was lots of food, and bottles and bottles of beer and wine. Sungura got a bit drunk. Some time after midnight Crocodile came up to Sungura and said, 'Sungura, my friend, it's too late to ferry you back to the mainland. Why don't you stay the night?'

'Marvelloush idea,' said Sungura. 'I'll shleep on the verandah. It'sh cool there.'

But it wasn't only the coolness Sungura was thinking of; he'd seen all Mrs Crocodile's eggs in a corner of the verandah. So, in the very early hours after the party

was over, Sungura got up and put all the eggs on the fire to roast them; about a dozen there were. When each egg was ready, he ate it and he didn't stop till he'd eaten up every egg. Then he lay down and went to sleep again.

The next morning after breakfast, Sungura said his goodbyes, climbed on Crocodile's back and they set off for the mainland.

When they were out in the middle of the river, Mrs Crocodile – still back at home – discovered that all her eggs were missing, and she shouted to her husband, 'Hey, Croccy, dear, Sungura's eaten all our eggs.'

Crocodile couldn't hear very well. 'What's that she said?' he asked Sungura on his back.

'She said, "Swim faster. A storm's coming".'

So Crocodile swam faster. Again Mrs Crocodile shouted out and this time Crocodile heard. He tipped Sungura off his back into the water and grabbed his leg in his mouth.

'Hey! *Woy! Woy!*' shouted Sungura. 'Catch my–*Woy!*–leg. That's a log–*Woy! Woy* – of wood you're holding. Look, there's my–*WOY! WOY!*–leg.'

And Crocodile let go of Sungura's leg and sank his teeth into a log of wood that was floating past. 'You've got me now, hold tight,' said Sungura.

And Sungura swam faster than he'd ever swum before to the shore. He limped out of the water and scrambled up the bank out of reach of Crocodile.

He'd saved his life but, of course, he'd lost another friend. And in fact, he gave up trying to make friends after that."

The storm's quite gone now and the sky's clear – millions of stars up there, twinkling pinholes in the black velvety night. After the rain everything smells fresh and wet. And there are hundreds of little gurgles as the rainwater runs down to the river. The insects are trilling and zizzing again; they won't stop till sunrise.

· 10 ·

Dubulihasa

"And who brought this wood?"

There's a number of us sitting all round the fire in Aunt's house – adults and a huddle of children, smaller children leaning against big ones and the smallest ones lying in laps. It's too cold to sit outside and very dark because it's a cloudy night. There's a glorious fire, just the sort of fire we need inside a house on a cold night; very little smoke and only an occasional flame. But it gives out a steady, bright glow of warmth and light. Somewhere somebody's found the right kind of wood and carried it back.

"Who brought this wood?" Aunt asks again. "Whoever it was, I thank you from the bottom of my heart. I thought this kind of wood was finished around here. I haven't seen it for years. I've been burning that sparky stuff that sets your thatch on fire."

Over our heads the thatched roof rises in a cone, supported by its framework of rafters; they look like a giant cobweb spanning the whole house. The fire glows and flickers, sending our shadows, twice as big as ourselves, over the walls and cobweb roof.

Masibani says, "I think it was the children who found it when they were herding cattle far from here.

130

They asked me to help them carry it back."

"Thank you," says Aunt. "So, you were herding, were you? Well then, I'll tell you a tale about herding, about a boy and his marvellous ox, Dubulihasa."

There's a stir from the huddle. It starts to sway and murmur, "Dubulihasa, Dubulihasa ambled along, ambled along."

Aunt grins and raises her arms, "Wait!" she says. "The tale hasn't come out as far as that yet."

Behind her on the wall and right up the cobweb roof the fire throws an enormous black shadow that looks like an ox with wide-spreading horns. And the cricket that lives under the corn-basket chirps to us busily, telling us it lives in this house too.

Aunt says, "The tale begins here. It goes like this –

There was a boy who used to herd cattle – a large number of cows, many young ones and an ox, a magnificent beast with a pair of horns that spread and rose from its head like arms. And the name of this ox was Dubulihasa.

Every day the boy used to herd his cattle. In the evening he used to take them back home and every morning he would take them out again.

One day, as the boy was looking after the cattle, a strange man came and said, 'Boy, follow me!'

The boy was afraid and said nothing. The man said, 'Follow me! And bring your cattle, especially that big ox!'

But the boy ran away before the man could catch him and, when he came back, the man had gone but the cattle were still there.

Three days later the strange man returned and this time he had a large macheté. He grabbed the boy before he could escape and said, 'There's no way out for you today. I'll kill you if you don't get that ox moving.' And the man tried to get Dubulihasa moving himself.

But Dubulihasa wouldn't move. He just stood like a rock and didn't move forward or back. He didn't move left or right.

The man said, 'If you don't get your ox moving, I'll kill you.' And he waved the macheté over the boy's head.

So the boy went up to Dubulihasa and he sang:

'Dubulihasa, Dubulihasa,
can you go on, now,
Dubulihasa?
Surely you heard how
he's going to kill me,
Dubulihasa?'

And Dubulihasa said, 'Mpoooo! Mpoooo!'
And he moved. He moved.
Dubulihasa ambled along, ambled along.
Dubulihasa dawdled along, dawdled along,
over the ground, up to the top of a hill.
And he stopped.
At the top of a hill he stopped.

The man said, 'Boy, get your ox moving again.'
The boy went up to Dubulihasa and he sang:

'Dubulihasa, Dubulihasa,
can you go on, now,
Dubulihasa?
Surely you heard how
he's going to kill me,
Dubulihasa?'

'Mpoooo! Mpoooo!'
And he moved. He moved.
Dubulihasa ambled along, ambled along.
Dubulihasa dawdled along, dawdled along,
over the ground, down to the bank of a river.
And he stopped.
On the bank of a river he stopped.

The man said, 'Boy, get your ox moving again.'
The boy went up to Dubulihasa and he sang:

'Dubulihasa, Dubulihasa,
please can you cross, now,
Dubulihasa?
Surely you heard how
he's going to kill me,
Dubulihasa?'

'Mpoooo! Mpoooo!'
And he moved. He crossed the river.
Dubulihasa ambled along, ambled along.
Dubulihasa dawdled along, dawdled along,
over the ground,
up to the gate in front of the man's cattleyard.
And he stopped.

134

At the gate into the man's cattleyard he stopped.

The man said, 'Boy, get your ox moving again.'
The boy went up to Dubulihasa and he sang:

'Dubulihasa, Dubulihasa,
can you go in, now,
Dubulihasa?
Surely you heard how
he's going to kill me,
Dubulihasa?'

'Mpoooo! Mpoooo!'
And he moved. He entered the yard.
Dubulihasa ambled along, ambled along.
Dubulihasa dawdled along, dawdled along,
over the ground, right to the middle of the cattleyard.
And he stopped.
In the middle of the cattleyard he stopped.
And he wee'd.

The man said, 'Boy, get your ox moving again.'
The boy went up to Dubulihasa and he sang:

'Dubulihasa, Dubulihasa,
can you go on, now,
Dubulihasa?
Surely you heard how
he's going to kill me,
Dubulihasa?'

Mpoooo! Mpoooo!

135

And he moved. He moved.
Dubulihasa ambled along, ambled along.
Dubulihasa dawdled along, dawdled along,
over the ground,
up to the gate in front of the cattle pen.
And he stopped.
At the gate into the cattle pen he stopped.

The man said, 'Boy, get your ox moving again.'
The boy went up to Dubulihasa and he sang:

'Dubulihasa, Dubulihasa,
can you go in, now,
Dubulihasa?
Surely you heard how
he's going to kill me,
Dubulihasa?'

Mpoooo! Mpoooo!
And he moved. Dubulihasa entered the pen
and he stood, stamping his hoofs and tossing his horns.
He stood.

The man brought some ropes and tried to tie the ox,
but he couldn't because Dubulihasa wouldn't stand
still.

The man said, 'Boy, tell your ox to keep still so I can
tie it.'
The boy went up to Dubulihasa and he sang:

'Dubulihasa, Dubulihasa,

136

> can you keep still, now,
> Dubulihasa?
> Surely you heard how
> he's going to kill me,
> Dubulihasa?'

> Mpoooo! Mpoooo!
> And Dubulihasa stood still.
> Still he stood.

The man tied him tight. Then the man took his macheté and tried to kill the ox. But he couldn't. He couldn't kill Dubulihasa.

The man said, 'Boy, tell your ox to be killed so we can cook it.'
The boy went up to Dubulihasa and he sang:

> 'Dubulihasa, Dubulihasa,
> can you be killed, now,
> Dubulihasa?
> Surely you heard how
> he's going to kill me,
> Dubulihasa?'

> Mpoooo! Mpoooo!
The man killed Dubulihasa.
He skinned him and took his hide right off. Then the man tried to shove a big stick through the body so they could roast it over the fire. But the stick wouldn't go through. No matter how hard the man pushed, the stick – wouldn't – go – through – the carcass.

The man said, 'Boy, tell your ox to be cooked so we can eat it.'

The boy went up to the carcass and he sang:

> 'Dubulihasa, Dubulihasa,
> can you be cooked, now,
> Dubulihasa?
> Surely you heard how
> he's going to kill me,
> Dubulihasa?'

The stick entered the body. They lifted the carcass over the fire and turned it round and round till it was cooked. When it was ready, they began to eat. But there was an old woman there who couldn't eat. The meat choked her and wouldn't go down.

The man said, 'Boy, tell your ox to be eaten.'

The boy went up to the meat and he sang:

> 'Dubulihasa, Dubulihasa,
> can you go down, now,
> Dubulihasa?
> Surely you heard how
> he's going to kill me,
> Dubulihasa?'

And the old woman chewed her meat and swallowed it. They ate and ate and ate till all the meat was finished and the bones were scattered all over the

place. The boy got up and collected all the bones into a pile in the corner of the yard.

When they'd finished eating, the man and his friends went off to the river to wash the grease off their hands. Only the boy and the old woman were left behind. The boy gave the old woman some tobacco. She put it in her pipe and started smoking. But after a while her head began nodding and soon she was fast asleep.

The boy got up and went to the pile of bones. One by one he picked them up and stuck them together with mud and cow dung from the yard. He stuck them all together, every one, even the little bones in the tail. He took the hide and threw it over the body — horns and hoofs and tail and all.

Then the boy went up to the body and he sang:

'Dubulihasa, Dubulihasa,
can you get up, now,
Dubulihasa?
Surely you heard how
he's going to kill me,
Dubulihasa?'

Mpoooo! Mpoooo!
Dubulihasa rose and tossed his horns,
stamped his hoofs and swished his tail,
swish to the left and swish to the right.
Dubulihasa rose and stood.

The boy climbed on Dubulihasa's back and held his
horns. He bent forward and sang into Dubulihasa's ear:

'Dubulihasa, Dubulihasa,
can you go home, now,
Dubulihasa?
Surely you heard how
he's going to kill me,
Dubulihasa?'

Mpoooo! Mpoooo!
And he moved. Dubulihasa was moving.
He trotted along, trotted along.
Dubulihasa plodded along, plodded along,
out of the yard, over the river, up the hill,
all the way back to the boy's home.
And he stopped.
Dubulihasa stopped and the boy climbed down.

'Where have you been all this time?' asked his mother.

The boy said, 'A man took Dubulihasa and me away.' And the boy told them everything that had happened.

And I can tell you, the joy in that house was great that night. There was eating and dancing, and drinking and singing.

Yiri-yiri-yiri-yiiii! Yiri-yiri-yiri-yiiii!

The tale is told. The tale is told."

· 11 ·

Omutugwa

The usual afternoon thunderstorm has passed. The night sky is clear and the moon is out. The whole world is shades of silver with black tree shapes, black house shapes, black people shapes and just black shapes. After the rain the air is fresh and damp. Louder than the unending noise from the night insects the African cuckoo is calling, calling, calling:

"*Ga-sia-noo!* Work-is-here! *Ga-sia-noo! Ga-sia-noo!*"

On a magic night like this after the day's work and school everybody is outside, making themselves a holiday. Men's voices, women's voices and children's voices echo all over our small valley. The church people are singing hymns. Even Mgadi, drunkard as usual, is singing hymns on his way home, teasing the church people:

"Hallelujah – hallelujah – hallebaloojah – hallebaloojah!"

Surely tomorrow they will try their best to save him from sin. But his wife will quarrel him first. There is her voice, loud, loud, loud from her compound, telling us all what she thinks of her husband:

"Neighbours! When they married me off, it was a man they said they would bring me. Now what do I do surely? Can you hear that drunkard thing, how he is staggering along like a baby? And like a baby all night long he will make his wee-wees over me and my house. Don't I have my own babies? Do I need another one?"

At the other end of our valley the young people are having a dance:

Doom-de. Doom-de. Doom-de. Doom-de.
Doom-de. Doom-de.

Grandmother says, "I will tell you a tale about the *omutugwa*, the servant girl, who nearly missed to go to the dance."

We are very many listening to Grandmother tonight; even some neighbours have come and Fanice, our cousin, who stays here and works for us. She is looking really smart tonight.

"You know what an *omutugwa* does, isn't it?" Grandmother says to Fanice.

"I know," says Fanice. "I bring the water and the firewood, I wash the clothes, I prepare the vegetables, I cook, I . . . "

"That is a lot of work for a small girl. Can you read and write?"

"I can't," says Fanice. "I don't usually go to school."

"You should go," says Grandmother. "You can't expect to be lucky like the servant girl in this story.

"That servant girl worked for one of those women who don't take care of their home or their families. In actual fact, the home was very tidy. But that was because of the *omutugwa*. That one was a good worker. Even, she looked after herself very nicely. She was having only one dress: an old, old, old school uniform. But it was always clean and well ironed, and all the torn parts were neatly sewn.

And the woman she worked for: that one was having two grown-up daughters and those ones resembled the mother: real bush children. Not even the servant girl could be able to make them look smart. They looked as if they had stayed with dirt for centuries and their hair was lumpy like grass after cows have slept on it.

One morning the two daughters said, 'We went to a fantastic dance last night – Congolese music. And the chief's son was there; that one is really up-to-date. But he didn't want to dance with us.'

The mother said, 'But you should have danced with him. Don't you admire to become the chief's daughter-in-law?'

'Even me: can I go to the dance next time?' asked the *omutugwa*.

The mother and the daughters laughed, and the mother said, 'Just look at this thing! So you think you are a girl to dance with the chief's son, is it? You are not going. You are here to work.'

A week passed and the time there was another dance was the time the mother gave the servant girl work to do. 'Hey, you girl! You come! That sack of millet in the kitchen: you pick all the stones before tomorrow morning,' said the mother to the *omutugwa*.

> "Oh!" interrupts Fanice in dismay.
> "That is a terrible job! Surely
> that is not fair."

144

"No, it is not fair, my
child," says Grandmother. "You can
take many days to pick stones from a
sack of millet. You know how small
millet grains are, isn't it?"
"I know," says Fanice. "You lose
them under your fingernail. That poor
girl! She really suffered!"
"Fani-wé," says Grandmother, "I
can see you have finished your work.
You are looking really smart. Are you
going to that dance down there?"
Fanice looks away and giggles but
says nothing. We can hear the drums:
Doom-de. Doom-de. Doom-de.
Doom-de.

The two daughters went to the dance and the mother
went to another place. But the *omutugwa*: that one
dragged and dragged and draaagged the sack of millet to
the door to pick the stones while the sun was setting.
With a huge sigh she poured some little millet out of
the sack on to a tray and with another HHuuge sigHH
she began looking for tiny, tiny, tiny, tiny stones among
the millet. She had known she wouldn't be able to go
to the dance.

But when she was just there picking stones, pick-
pick-pick-picking . . .

Yi! . . .

From out of the sky a thousand magic things came
fluttering down around her head. All the birds, from

145

the smallest to the largest, came from miles around to pick the stones out of the millet.

They were all there: the gorgeous sunbirds; the finches and the yellow weaver birds: those ones were the hardest workers. The cuckoo, *Igasi-yi-hano*, was there, calling all the other birds to work:

'*Ga-sia-noo! Ga-sia-noo! Ga-sia-noo! Ga-sia-noo!*'

The brilliant starlings came, the thrushes, the robins. The pied crows were there and even the brown kites. The noisy ibises, the white cattle egrets, and taller than them all the beautiful crowned cranes.

The yard was a patchwork carpet of jostling bird backs. And the *omutugwa* was busy gathering the grain which the birds had picked, and pouring out more, more, more, more, mooore.

The work was finished *kabisa* – done completely – in less time than you take to prepare a meal and away the birds flew. The sack was full of grains of millet and a heap of tiny stones was lying by the door.

But the magic was not finished yet.

When the *omutugwa* went to the bathroom to wash herself . . .

Yi! . . .

Clothes were just there on the floor, lovely, lovely clothes. And a pair of shoes.

She washed and dressed herself and rubbed her skin with oil to make it shine. Then the busy weaver birds returned. Twisting, tying, pecking, knotting with their beaks, those ones plaited on her head a wonderful design.

When she was ready, she did not resemble an *omutugwa*. Beautiful as a crowned crane, she had been

146

changed into a girl to capture the eyes of the chief's son! *kabisa!*

And surely, the time she entered that place where the dance was is exactly the time the eyes of the chief's son stuck to her. And they danced together as the cranes dance – dance – dance – and – dance, until the evening was nearly to an end.

But she had known she must reach home before the mother and daughters, otherwise they would quarrel her. They would refuse her food, or, even worse, they would chase her away and then she would not be having a job.

So, when she saw the dance was nearly to end, she said to the chief's son, 'I must go now. Goodbye!' And she ran away into the night, quick, quick, like a ground jet.

'Yi! Come back! Come back!' shouted the chief's son in surprise.

'I can't. They will quarrel me at home.' And she ran, ran, raaaan. But as she was running, one of her shoes fell off. The chief's son stopped to pick it up. When he stood up straight again, having the shoe in his hand, she had disappeared *kabisa.*

The next morning the mother asked the daughters, 'And last night: did you dance with the chief's son?'

Those ones replied, 'We were just going to dance, but a small girl came in late. She looked a bit like this one here, but beautiful, much more beautiful. And the chief's son danced with that one all, all, all, all the time. And the rest of us: not one, not a single one was chosen.'

The *omutugwa* said nothing. That one was just

walking there in her old school uniform and bare feet, as usual.

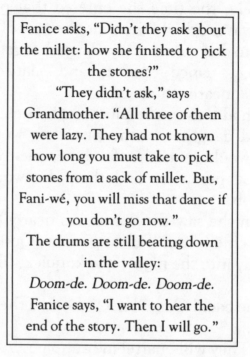

Fanice asks, "Didn't they ask about the millet: how she finished to pick the stones?"

"They didn't ask," says Grandmother. "All three of them were lazy. They had not known how long you must take to pick stones from a sack of millet. But, Fani-wé, you will miss that dance if you don't go now."

The drums are still beating down in the valley:

Doom-de. Doom-de. Doom-de.

Fanice says, "I want to hear the end of the story. Then I will go."

In actual fact, the chief's son was very upset. He did not know who that girl was, or where she lived. All he was having was the shoe which she had lost when she was running away like a ground jet. So he called the *askaris*, the chief's guards, and said to them, 'I met a girl at the dance last night. I don't know her name, or where she lives. But that one is the girl I admire to marry. This is her shoe. Go and call all the young girls here, then we can know which one fits into this shoe.'

So the *askaris* went and announced all round the district, 'All unmarried girls must report to the chief's house now! All unmarried girls must report to the chief's house now!'

When the mother heard this, she said to the two daughters, 'How can you miss this chance to become the chief's daughter-in-law? Go! Go! Go! Go and marry the son.'

'Even me: can I go to the house?' asked the *omutugwa*.

'You! You were not there,' said the mother. 'The son of a chief does not admire to marry an *omutugwa* like you. You remain here and work.'

When the daughters came back, the mother asked them, 'What happened, my daughters?'

And the daughters replied, 'He is having a shoe that belongs to the girl he admires to marry. The girl who fits into the shoe: that one is the girl he is going to marry.'

'And you: did you fit in?'

One of the daughters said, 'I tried; I tried; I tri-i-i-ied. I really tried. But one of my toes is too long.'

'Too long! Cut it off!'

GU-DOO

'WOY!'

Then the mother went with the daughter to the chief's house. Poor child! That one without a toe was limp-limp-limping along behind her mother. But when they reached there, the chief's son refused her to put on the shoe.

'I don't want a girl without a toe,' he said. 'Take her away.'

When they reached home, the mother said to the second daughter, 'And you: did you fit in?'

The second daughter replied, 'I fitted in; I really fitted. But my heel was out.'

'*Yi!* Your heel! Is it only a heel that prevents me to become the mother of the chief's daughter-in-law? Cut it off!'

GU-DOO

'WOY!'

Then the mother went with the second daughter to the chief's house. And this one without a heel was limping even worse than that one without a toe. But when they reached there, the chief's son just looked at the girl and said, 'Now surely, this is just what I was refusing. I don't want a girl who is having no toe, and I don't want a girl who is having no heel. I want my girl: that lost one.'

But it defeated the chief's son *kabisa* to find the girl who would fit into the shoe. So he decided to announce another dance to find the girl who was missing.

And the day of the dance is the very day the *omutugwa* was surprised again by the same magic as that one before. The two daughters had gone to the dance; the one was having no toe and the other was having no heel. And the mother had said to the *omutugwa*, 'That other sack of millet in the kitchen: you pick all the stones before tomorrow.' And then the mother just left the *omutugwa* there, alone in the house.

Then, just as before, all the birds came from miles and miles and miles around to pick the stones from the millet.

Igasi-yi-hano, the cuckoo, was calling, calling, calling:

'*Ga-sia-noo! Ga-sia-noo! Ga-sia-noo! Ga-sia-noo!*'

All, all, all, they all came: the gorgeous sunbirds

150

with their long beaks; the finches; the yellow weaver
birds: those ones never stop weaving themselves new
nests; the starlings in their brilliant colours; the
thrushes; the robins: those ones like singing duets; the
pied crows; the brown kites; the noisy ibises; the cattle
egrets, whiter than snow; and the crowned cranes, the
most beautiful of them all.

It was magic!

Quick, quick, quick the birds picked the stones out
of the millet and flew away. When the *omutugwa* had
finished washing and dressing herself, the weaver birds
returned to make her hair tidy again.

And – she – was – ready!

And the moment the *omutugwa* reached the dance is
the moment the chief's son recognized her:

'*Ehéee*! This is the girl I have been looking for. This

151

is the girl I am going to marry.' And he began to put the shoe on her foot. Surely, it fitted her *kabisa*.

Then he went with the girl to his father, the chief, and said, 'Father, this is the girl whose shoe fell off. This is the girl I admire to marry.'

'So, you have found her at last,' said his father. 'Now I will go and speak to her parents and prepare for the wedding.'

And the time everybody had known that a wedding feast would soon take place was the time for each and every person — except the mother and her two daughters — to be happy. The women shrilled:

Yiri-yiri-yiri-yiiii! Yiri-yiri-yiri-yiiii!

And that was how the *omutugwa* was married to the chief's son."

"Fanice, now you can go to your dance," says Grandmother. The drums are still beating down in the valley. Fanice stands up. She smoothes her dress and we all start teasing her.

"Fani-wé, who plaited your hair, the birds?"

"Fani-wé, make sure you walk where the eyes of the chief's son will stick to you."

"Leave your shoe behind so he can know who you are."

And Fanice walks off into the moonlight, following the call of *Igasi-yi-hano*:

Ga-sia-noo! Ga-sia-noo! Ga-sia-noo!

·12·

The Wise Little Girl

In some parts of Africa if you glide on wide wings, as vultures do, looping slowly through the sky, you will see nothing on the earth below you.

Well, not nothing really. Scattered around there are trees and sand and grass. And more sand and grass and trees. And trees and sand and . . . All around in every direction. Nothing different. Nowhere to stop. No hills, no valleys. No people. May be some wild animals, but no people. No signs of people. No fields, no houses, no roads. NO PEOPLE.

Enormous, empty freedom. And the freedom and emptiness are frightening if you're used to living with hedges and houses. We call these parts:

DESERT – BUSH – THIRSTLANDS

And we frighten ourselves with these names:

THIRSTLANDS

But there are people there – just a few, moving around beneath the trees. And for these people this is home. Just as safe and familiar for them as the High Street is for us. And just as dangerous too.

If you fly at night, you can see their fires – just one or two, flickering in the darkness that's so thick you can feel it like black paint wrinkling across your eyeballs and your forehead.

There's a fire. Let's drop in, shall we? And listen.
Down through the darkness –
down – down – down – down –
fruuuu – fruuu – fruu – fru – frufrufrufru. And –
here we are.

In this tiny egg of shifting, twickering firelight we sit among people – parents and children and grandparents; uncles and aunts and cousins – and listen. And turn our backs to the fearful darkness that stretches all round us as far as – as far as fear and much further. Only the stars overhead are near; twinkling pinholes in the ceiling; millions of them, like sparkling ashdust on black velvet, noiselessly drifting through the darkness up there.

Behind our backs a hyena yelps, wildebeest snort and far off from time to time a lion roars. And the whole night's loud with crickets trilling.

Grandma's talking: "It isn't only wild animals you should be careful of; it's people too, especially strange men. I'll tell you the tale of the little girl who was wiser than the older girls.

Once upon a time a nice young woman went out to the onion place. She went to dig up wild onions. And she put a flower in her hair, a pretty flower, a red one. And then she reached the onion place and she started digging with her digging stick.

Then some young men come. And one of the young men is blind in one eye. She's never seen them before. They are nice young men; they help her dig up onions.

154

*Choom – choom – choom – choom –
choom – choom.*

Come on! Help them dig up the onions. You're nice
young people too, aren't you?
Choom – choom – choom.

That's right. Well done. They find lots of onions. Her
bag's soon full. Then the man – the one-eyed man –
says, 'Tell your friends to come and tomorrow we'll
have a party.'

'All right,' says the young woman. Then she goes
home with her bag of onions. And she says to her
friends, 'Look at all the onions I've found. Let's go and
dig some more tomorrow.' And then she goes to bed.

The next morning she picks a fresh flower, another
red one, and puts it in her hair. Then she starts out for
the onion place with her friends. And they all take
their digging sticks.

But a little girl goes with them. And one of the older girls says to the little girl, 'You stay here. Go and help your mother. We don't want to carry you.'

Then the little girl's big sister says, 'She'll be all right. Let her come. She's grown up now and can run by herself. We don't need to put her in a baby-sling any longer.' And the little girl goes with them.

And they reach the onion place and they begin to dig.

Choom – choom – choom – choom – choom – choom.

Then the little girl sees lots of footprints in the sand, all over the place. And she goes to the young woman – the one with the pretty flower – and says, 'I thought you were alone here yesterday. There's lots of footprints all over the place. Who was with you?'

And the young woman says, 'Nobody. I was alone. I walked everywhere, looking for onions.'

But the little girl knows she's lying. She knows they are men's footprints. Then she looks around again and she sees a big hole – a hole where an anteater used to live.

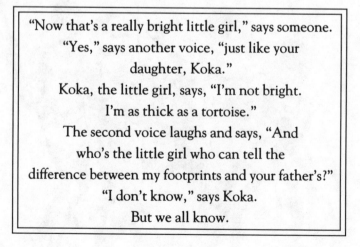

"Now that's a really bright little girl," says someone.

"Yes," says another voice, "just like your daughter, Koka."

Koka, the little girl, says, "I'm not bright. I'm as thick as a tortoise."

The second voice laughs and says, "And who's the little girl who can tell the difference between my footprints and your father's?"

"I don't know," says Koka.

But we all know.

The little girl isn't happy. She keeps on jumping up. She stops digging and she goes on a prowl. And on one of her prowls she sees a group of men. They're squatting in a circle with their heads together, talking. And they don't see her.

Then she goes back to the older girls and one of them says, 'Proper little fidget you are. Make me quite nervous. Just stay still and help us dig or I'll smack you.'

The little girl says nothing. She just digs and digs and keeps on looking round. Then she sees the men coming near. The man with one blind eye is first and he's playing a little pipe. The little girl knows the tune and the words and she feels shivery and a bit scared.

> 'Here it is.
> *More blood:*
> Here it is.
> *More blood.'*

Then the older girls start dancing with the men. They leave their digging sticks with their onion bags and they dance with the strange men. But the little girl doesn't dance. She walks about among the other girls. And she whispers to them, 'That tune: listen to it. Don't you know the words? Stop! Please stop! Please!' But they wouldn't stop. They wouldn't listen.

They say to her, 'Oh, what a baby you are! Go away and play by yourself. You'll know about all this when you get older.' And they just go on dancing with the men, dancing to the music —

more blood — more blood — more blood — more blood

And they forget all about her. And the little girl joins them. She starts dancing too. And she ties her skirt to her sister's skirt.

And the music's getting wilder and wilder –

more blood – moreblood –
morebloodmorebloodmorebloodmore

And the girls are getting really excited. And the noise is getting really loud. And the girls are shrilling and really screaming:

Yiri-yiri-yiri-yiiii. Yiri-yiri-yiri-yiiii.

The dust's thick. Arms, heads like grinning masks, popeyes and snarling teeth. Legs jerk, jerk, jerking up and down.

Then the little girl says to her sister, 'Our skirts are tangled up. Come and sit down behind that bush so I can untie them.'

And they go and sit down behind the bush and the little girl says, 'That music: are you sure you don't know the words?'

And her sister says, 'No, I've never heard it before. Isn't it fantastic?'

The little girl says, 'But it means they're looking for our blood. Those men are looking for more blood – our blood! Come on! Let's run away before it's too late. Come on!' Then they run away from the dancing. And the little girl runs backwards behind her sister. She's running backwards and putting her feet in her sister's footprints. Then they run to the anteater hole and go inside. And it looks as if somebody's walked away from the hole. But really they're inside the hole, hiding.

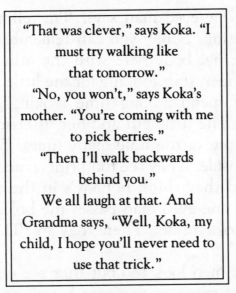

"That was clever," says Koka. "I
must try walking like
that tomorrow."
"No, you won't," says Koka's
mother. "You're coming with me
to pick berries."
"Then I'll walk backwards
behind you."
We all laugh at that. And
Grandma says, "Well, Koka, my
child, I hope you'll never need to
use that trick."

Then the pipe stops playing and they hear different
noises. Lots of thumping and shouting and razor-blade
screams.

And then silence.

And then a really funny noise: a sort of slurpy,
sucking noise. And then some licky noises.

And the little girl's sister says, 'Oh, my poor friends!
Let me go and help them.'

The little girl holds her skirt and says, 'Quiet! Do
you think you'd have lived if you'd been there too?'
They crouch in the anteater hole and listen.

There's silence again.

Then they hear one of the men speaking, the man
with one blind eye. He says, 'There are two girls
missing: the very young one and the beautiful one – the
one I was dancing with.'

The other men say, 'Don't listen to him. He can't
see. He only has one eye.'

And the one-eyed man says, 'I'm telling you: two girls are missing. Surely you can remember the child. Can you see her body here with the others?'

Then the men start looking for the little girl and her sister. They spend a long time looking. They look everywhere. The little girl and her sister see their legs passing in front of the hole many times. But the men don't look inside. They see footprints going away from the hole and they think nobody's in there.

Then the one-eyed man passes the hole. He kneels down and looks inside. 'There they are. They're in the hole.'

The other men look too but they see nothing. The little girl just manages to cover herself and her sister with cobwebs.

Then one of the young men sticks his spear down the hole and it cuts the big girl's heel. The little girl warns her sister to keep quiet and quickly wipes the blood off the spear point.

Then the one-eyed man looks in the hole again and he sees the little girl's eyes shining at him. And he says, 'There she is. Look!'

'Ya! Give over!' the other men say. 'You and your girls in anteater holes!' And they walk way. Then they say, 'We're thirsty after all that dancing and drinking. We're going off to the water hole for a drink. You stay here and find your two girls. We'll bring you some water.' And off they go.

The man with one blind eye sits down by the anteater hole. Then the little girl sings very quietly to him from inside the hole. She sings in a tiny, squeaky voice, like the spirits use when they speak.

'Killed them all.
Murder.
Made them fall.
Murder.
Time to drink.
Murder.
Water's best.
Murder.
Take a rest.
Murder.'

And the one-eyed man says to himself, 'Mmm! Why not? I am thirsty.' And he goes away too.

Then the little girl and her sister come out of the hole and the older sister can't walk by herself. Her heel's injured. The little girl has to help her. They can't walk far like that; the little girl's only small; she's only a child really. She can only move very slowly. Her sister's heavy and she's leaning on her. They're moving so slowly past a red flower lying on the sand.

Then the men come back. They see the girls and they start running towards them. 'There they are! After them!' the men shout.

Oh dear! This is the end for sure. Help! Help! Murder! They're going to catch the girls. Help!

I know. I have an idea. Can you help me with this spell? This magic spell? Can you? I can't do it by myself. It needs two of us. Can you help me with this spell. . .? . . .

Good! Come on, then, there's no time to waste. You say, 'Change it!' Got it? 'Change it!' Good! And I'll say the magic words. Ready. . .? . . .

161

Here's a foot.
"Change it!"
Here's a leg.
"Change it!"
Here's a chest.
"Change it!"
Here's an arm.
"Change it!"
Here's a head.
"Change it!"

Have we done it? Yes, I think the magic's worked.
Look! We've turned the girls into trees. Well done!
Two thorn trees. And look! See those drops of gum
round the tree trunks like sticky sweets. They were the
beads the girls were wearing round their waists.

Then the men reach the trees and they're mystified;
totally befoozled. Well, you would be too, wouldn't
you? One moment running after somebody and the
next time you blink you see two trees. The men walk
round and round the two thorn trees, scratching their
heads. And one of them scratches a gum drop off one of
the trees and puts it in his mouth.

'Mmm! Good this. Here, you try,' he says. And he
gives some drops to all his friends. And they all stand
around picking off the gum drops, sucking and chewing, chewing and sucking.

Then the young men start yawning and sighing and
rubbing their eyes. And then one after the other they
just flop on the ground. They lie sprawling anyhow all
over the place. They're all asleep, put to sleep by the
gum drops.

Sh! Quietly now! We mustn't wake them up. Right, now what we have to do is change those trees back into girls. You've done it once. Do you think you can do another magic spell with me. . . ? . .

Here's a root.
"Change it!"
Here's a trunk.
"Change it!"
Here's a branch.
"Change it!"
Here's a twig.
"Change it!"
Here's a leaf.
"Change it!"

Have we done it? Ah yes, look! There they are again, the little girl and her sister. And look, even her heel's better now. Well done!

Then the little girl and her sister spread lots of sticky gum all over the men's eyes, so that they can't open their eyes when they wake up.

And then they run off and reach their village safely.

So, children, you just let this tale be a lesson to you: just take care wherever you are. Keep your eyes open and your wits about you. It doesn't matter if you've been to a place every day for years and years; just take care each time you go there. You never know what's going to happen, do you?"

When Grandma stops talking, the only sound is the crickets trilling everywhere.

And it's time for us to fly away.

Off! Up and away into the darkness, under the millions of stars.

Do you see Grandma and her family sitting down there round their tiny nightlight fire? There they sit every night, in the shadowy firelight, with stars in their ceiling and shadows for walls. And as they talk and tell stories, the breeze from the desert blows their words away into the night.

·13·

The Two Swindlers

Let's go to a town in Africa and follow Hassan and his little sister, Sadiya. She's only six; such an independent little thing, walking there in front all by herself. She always refuses to take anybody's hand.

They're off to listen to the adults telling stories. It's evening; up there in the sky the moon's a grapefruit lantern. Down here in the street the seethrough moonlight flattens everything to passing shadows. Silver clouds rise round people's feet as they walk through the dry dust and their voices echo from the high, dark walls of the houses on each side. Hassan throws a stone at a small, lumpy shadow near a wall. The shadow takes the shape of a dog and drifts away into the darkness. Hassan doesn't like strange, town dogs ever since one bit him in the leg a few weeks ago.

Sadiya's going on fast – half trotting, half plodding, the way that small children walk. She knows where to go. She's leading us towards the murmur of people talking.

Come on, quickly now, or we'll lose her in the crowd. There she goes, right into the middle of a crowd of people sitting just off the street. They're scattered about in small, friendly groups, the oldest people

166

sitting on a couple of long tree trunks, the other adults and children sitting on the ground, talking and laughing with their neighbours.

Hassan sits down next to Sadiya and a voice says, "*Sannu*, Hassan! *Sannu*, Sadiya! So you've come."

"*Sannu*, Uncle," says Hassan. "Yes, we've come to listen to the stories."

A voice from the crowd shouts out, "Usman, when are we going to hear your words of wisdom?"

Another voice says, "Usman, creator of dreams, tell us a story."

Uncle says to Hassan and Sadiya, "We've had two stories already; they weren't very good. Usman is the best story-teller of us all."

Another voice says, "Usman, are you awake? Give him a nudge somebody."

And at last Usman speaks, "People, I'm awake. All my stories slink off like kicked dogs with their tails between their legs after those two magnificent stories we've just heard."

"Usman! Now I know you're sleeping. Shall I kick you till we get a story from you?"

"No, no, friends, don't be hard on me," says Usman, laughing. "Rather than kicks, here's a tale, a tale for you: the two swindlers. You will help me with it, won't you?"

"Let it come out," says everyone in delight. "The swindlers: that one's the best. Of course we'll help you. Begin! We're listening." And there's a slight rustling as everybody settles to listen, then silence.

"Well then, here we go. One swindler was a tall,

brown-skinned man from Kano, with smooth, plump cheeks; well-fed, well-clothed, well-spoken. You wouldn't think him a swindler, but he was the sharpest in Kano.

The other swindler was from Katsina. He was a shortish, bony, black-skinned man with jerky, freeze-frame movements like a squirrel. And like a squirrel he was always hiding things in secret places.

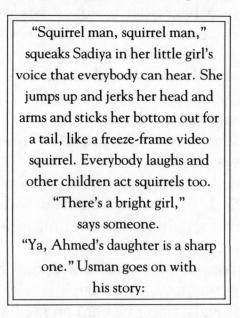

"Squirrel man, squirrel man," squeaks Sadiya in her little girl's voice that everybody can hear. She jumps up and jerks her head and arms and sticks her bottom out for a tail, like a freeze-frame video squirrel. Everybody laughs and other children act squirrels too.
"There's a bright girl," says someone.
"Ya, Ahmed's daughter is a sharp one." Usman goes on with his story:

Well, one day these two swindlers were both short of money – bills piling up, wives demanding money for this and money for that. You know how it is. So the two swindlers each set about making a dishonest *naira* or two.

Our man from Kano went out into the bush to an enormous baobab tree and he tore a large strip of bark off its trunk. The Kano man took the bark back to town and went to the round pits where cloth is dyed.

He put the bark into a dyeing pit and dyed it deep blue. Then he found a round stone and beat the bark to make it soft and loose like cloth.

It was hard work for our smooth-faced swindler from Kano:

> *Beat – mmm! Beat – mmm! Beat – mmm!*
> *Beat – mmm! Beat – mmm!*

Come on, help him. You said you'd help me with this story:

> *Beat – mmm! Beat – mmm! Beat – mmm!*
> *Beat – mmm!* That's right.

When he'd finished beating he dyed the bark once more to make it really dark and then let it dry in the sun. If you didn't look too closely, you'd have thought it was material for a pair of jeans. Finally, our man from Kano folded the bark in a piece of paper and set off for the market – well pleased with himself.

Meanwhile our man from Katsina wasn't idle. He took a goat-skin bag to a gravel pit and filled the bag with small round stones, nearly to the top. On top of the stones he spread money, two hundred white cowrie shells, hiding the stones underneath. Then he tied the mouth of his bag tightly and off he went to the market. And mighty pleased he was with himself too, was our sharp-faced Katsina man.

And on the road to the market our two swindlers met. There they were, toe to toe, face to face, the Kano man looking down at the Katsina man, and the Katsina man looking up at the Kano man.

The Kano man spoke first, '*Sannu*, my good fellow! Where are you heading for with that bag?'

The Katsina man replied, 'How do there, mate. I'm

for the market. And what about you with that parcel?'

'I say, my good man,' said the Kano man, 'this is a piece of frightfully good luck. I am going to the market too. You do not wish by any chance to buy a length of top quality dark blue cloth, do you?'

'That's just what I been looking for all this time,' said the Katsina man, 'a length of dark blue cloth for my next suit, you know. Here, mate, take this bag; twenty thousand cowries.'

'Done,' said the Kano swindler. Poker-faced, they exchanged the bag for the parcel, each trying not to show how delighted he was with his swindle. And they hurried off into the bushes on opposite sides of the road.

The short man from Katsina rushed behind the first bush, chuckling to himself, 'I done him. I done him. A new suit for two hundred cowries.' He rrripped the paper off the parcel and looked, and fingered, and looked again, and fingered it some more. Then he chucked it all away. 'That smart Alec from Kano. He done me! Dark blue cloth! That's baobab bark. I'll get him for this.'

Meanwhile on the other side of the road, the smooth-faced man from Kano pulled and jerked at the string round the mouth of the bag. 'Come on! Come on!' He couldn't untie it fast enough. Out shot a few white cowrie shells and then a flood of small, grey stones. 'Well, I'll be blowed,' said the Kano man. 'That fellow from Katsina has sold me down the river. He's sharper than I thought – almost as sharp as me. Twenty thousand cowries? Twenty thousand stones, more like.'

So, on opposite sides of the road the two swindlers

stood up, brushed down their clothes, smoothed their hair and fixed smiles on their faces, two wide crocodile grins, like this:

eeeeeeee!

And the two swindlers, the smooth-faced man from Kano and the short, bony man from Katsina, grinning like crocodiles:

eeeeeeee!

swaggered casually, so casually – out for a stroll, admiring the view, humming – casually back on the road. And there they were again, toe to toe, face to face, Kano crocodiling down at Katsina:

eeeeeeee!

and Katsina crocodiling up at Kano:

eeeeeeee!

Katsina spoke first, 'Who are you gawping at, smooth face?'

The Kano man said, 'I was always told, my good man, that staring is not frightfully good manners.'

The Katsina swindler relaxed a bit, stopped smiling and said, 'That was great, like. You nearly diddled me there. You're the sharpest man I know – not counting me, of course.'

The Kano man wasn't smiling either by now and he said, 'You have taken the very words out of my mouth, my good fellow. Real enterprise you have. A smart chap like you shouldn't be messing about with stones. Why don't you join me? We could make a fortune together.'

The Katsina man said, 'Great idea! You can't diddle me and I can't diddle you, no way. You're on.'

'Shake on it then. Gentleman's agreement,' said the

Kano man, wiping his hand.

'Oh, all right then,' said the Katsina man, wiping *his* hand. And the two gentlemen swindlers shook hands and then wiped their hands again.

So, here we go once more, folks: the tall man and the short man, walking along the road, looking for their first swindle.

And after a while our two swindlers came across some merchants camping by the road. It was a camel caravan that had just passed through the terrible dangers of the Sahara Desert, and now they had the bad luck to get in the way of our two swindlers – worse than a sandstorm in the Sahara Desert any day.

There were several tents, about a dozen merchants, twenty camels, and their loads piled up near the tents – blocks of salt, dates, rich brocade for clothes and copper bowls. Lovely loot for our two swindlers.

Kano crocodiled down at Katsina:

eeeeeee!

And Katsina crocodiled up at Kano:

eeeeeee!

They backed off before the merchants saw them and sat down behind a bush to decide what to do.

'We could make the camels run away, my good man,' said the Kano swindler.

'Don't act daft,' said the Katsina man. 'We can't scare twenty tired camels.'

'Well then, suppose we set fire to their tents tonight.'

'Is that the best you can do in Kano?' asked the

Katsina swindler. 'Look, fat face! Do you know the blind trick?'

'Why, of course,' said the Kano swindler. 'You have taken the words right out of my mouth. It was on the tip of my tongue to suggest it.' And the Kano man crocodiled down at the Katsina man:

eeeeeeee!

'Is that a fact?' said the Katsina man. 'Jolly good show, old fellow.' And he crocodiled up at the Kano man:

eeeeeeee!

The Kano man said, 'Now my good chap, let's go and find a calabash to use as a begging bowl the way that blind people do.'

So off they went to look for a calabash. And what do you know?

D–DNNNNN

Just at that moment what should come walking by but a . . . No, no! That won't do at all. I was just about to say that a calabash came walking by. But that's a crazy idea. You don't want calabashes walking around in this story, do you?"

"Oh yes, we do," says everybody.

"Oh no, you don't."

"Oh yes, we do."

"Oh no, you don't."

"Oh yes, we do."

"You do? You really do?"

"YES"

"All right then, have it your own way, you crazy lot. We tell this story together, you and I.

Let's go back a bit: so, off they went to look for a calabash. And what do you know?

D–DNNNNN

Just at that moment what should come walking by but a – CALABASH

Our two swindlers weren't a bit surprised to see a calabash walking down the road; such things happen every day in Kano and Katsina. They caught the calabash, cut it in half and then they had a begging bowl each, just like blind people carry around to beg for food and money. Then they lay down in the shade and slept till sunset.

When it was dark they closed their eyes and groped their way into the merchants' camp, holding their bowls in front and crying:

'Sadaka! Sadaka! Sadaka!

Take pity! Take pity! Take pity!'

The poor merchants suspected nothing and sat the swindlers down near the fire. They gave them food to eat and coffee to drink, and invited them to sleep in the camp. When all the merchants were asleep, all you could hear was:

snoring: *gh-gh-gh-gh-phew! gh-gh-gh-gh-phew!*

Come on then, snore a bit.

Camel chewing: *tut-tut-tut-tut-tut-tut-tut.*

Insects: *ting-eeee-urp-ting-zzzz.*

That's right, keep up the snoring, chewing and insecting, but quietly, or you won't hear the rest of the story.

MEANWHILE

our two swindlers opened their eyes and stood up very
quietly. They tiptoed to the pile of merchandise. The
Kano man picked up a roll of brocade:
Hup!
And the Katsina man picked up two copper bowls:
Hup!
Quickly they tiptoed out of the camp:
tip-toe tip-toe tip-toe tip-toe
to a disused well which they'd seen in the afternoon.
And they threw the brocade and the bowls down the
well:

Brrr. Kling-ting. Kling-ting. Brrr.
FLUMMMMM

And then back to the pile for more loot:
tip-toe tip-toe tip-toe tip-toe
And so on. And all the time there was the snoring, the
chewing and the insecting.

Right now, have you got that? You've got to help
them carry everything to the well.

Off you go, then!

Good, that's enough now.

They carried everything and threw it down the well;
all the brocade, all the bowls, all the salt, and nearly all
the dates – they ate a few on the way.

I expect you would've done the same, wouldn't you?
YOU THIEVES!

They hid a length of rope nearby and they even threw their begging bowls down the well.

When they'd done all that, they tip-toed – very tired now – back to the camp, lay down by the fire again and went to sleep. And all you could hear was:

> the snoring
> the chewing
> the insects.

The next morning I'm sure you can imagine what happened when the merchants discovered all their stuff was missing: the cafuffle, the hullabaloo in that camp.

> The lifting of stones
> the searching behind bushes
> the arm-raising to heaven
> the tearing of hair
> and more stone lifting
> more hair-tearing.

And the wailing – oh yes, the wailing. Wouldn't you wail if you'd lost everything?

Come on then, wail.

No, no, not like that. I'll have to teach you to wail properly.

Oh, my dates, my lovely dates, all gone:

> **Sniff-sniff. Boo-hoo.**

Oh, my salt, my lovely salt, all gone:

> **Sniff-sniff. Boo-hoo.**

Oh, my brocade, my lovely brocade, all gone:

> **Sniff-sniff. Boo-hoo.**

Oh, my copper bowls, my lovely copper bowls, all gone:

> **Sniff-sniff. Boo-hoo.**

Even the two swindlers were rushing around –

177

blindly, of course – bumping into people, wailing for their begging bowls which they'd thrown down the well.

Go on then, wail for the begging bowls:

Oh, my begging bowl, my lovely begging bowl, all gone:

Sniff-sniff. Boo-
SILENCE: ABSOLUTE SILENCE!
Cease that snivelling! Not another sniff more! Sh!

When the merchants heard the beggars wailing for their begging bowls, they stopped wailing themselves in amazement. They couldn't believe their ears. Then a great rage came over them and they all rushed at the two swindlers and pushed them out of the camp, shouting: 'Begging bowls? What about our brocade, and the copper bowls, the salt and the dates? What's a begging bowl to brocade? Clear off! Go on! We don't want you here.'

And our two swindlers ran off as quickly as they could. They ran away behind an ant-hill and flopped down, killing themselves with laughter.

They watched the merchants break up camp, get on their camels and ride off to find their merchandise.

Camel-walking noise now:

Sh-waa-ch-p. Sh-waa-ch-p. Sh-waa-ch-p.
Getting quieter now, because they're going away:
Sh-waa-ch-p. Sh-waa-ch-p.

MEANWHILE

back at the ant-hill our two swindlers stood up and walked over to the well. They looked down the well at their loot. Then they looked at each other. Then they looked down the well again. And they crocodiled at each other: the Kano man crocodiling down at Katsina:

eeeeeeee!

and Katsina crocodiling up at Kano:

eeeeeeee!

The Kano crocodile spoke first, through his teeth, 'My very good man, I think you should go down.'

eeeeeeee!

And the Katsina crocodile replied through his teeth, 'Not on your nelly, ta very much! After you, sir!'

eeeeeeee!

The Kano man said, 'No, I would rather not. I don't have a head for depths. You go down, there's a good sport.'

eeeeeeee!

And the Katsina man said, 'All right then, to cut the cackle, I'll go.' And he smiled a great crocodile smile from ear to ear:

eeeeeeeeeeeeeeee!

So, the Katsina man tied the rope round his middle and the Kano man lowered him down the well.

Down at the bottom the Katsina man started tying the rope to the first bundle, while at the top the Kano man was very pleased with life. He was actually smiling and humming a little tune:

'De-diddle-e-de! De-diddle-e-de! De-diddle-e-de!' He thought he'd won. But he hadn't as you'll see.

Up from the well came the Katsina man's voice, echoing:

'Heave-ho-o-o-o-o!'

The Kano man heaved the bundle up to the top:
>*'Hey-up! Hey-up! Hey-up!'*

He threw the rope back down the well:
>*Slither-slither-slither.*

He ran with the bundle to a bush:
>*Pa-ta-pa-ta-pa-ta-pa-ta.*

He dropped the bundle:
>*Flummm!*

He picked up a big stone:
>*'Hey-up!'*

He ran back to the well with the stone:
>*Pa-ta-pa-ta-pa-ta-pa-ta.*

He threw the stone down near the mouth of the well:
>*Flummm!*

And then the Katsina man's voice again:
>*'Heave-ho-o-o-o-o.'*

Right then, have you got all that? Let's get all those bundles up from the well. Off you go!

MEANWHILE

down in the well the Katsina man was wondering how to make sure the Kano man wouldn't leave him at the bottom. After a lot of work the Kano swindler looked down the well and said, 'You're doing a good job down there, old chap. Now, when you tie on the very last bundle, let me know, will you? You yourself will be the next bundle I pull up after that, and I want to take extra care pulling you up. I wouldn't want you to come to any harm, would I, my dear fellow?' And the Kano man crocodiled down at the pile of stones by the well:
>*eeeeeeee!*

180

A short while later the Katsina man called up the well, 'Hey, Lord Kano! This is the last bundle. It's extra big. I put two rolls of brocade in it.'

The Kano swindler said, 'Right you are, my good man. We'll soon have you out.' And he started pulling up the last bundle. It was very, very heavy:

Heeey-up! Heeey-up! Heeey-up! Heeey-up!

And he staggered with it to the other bundles:

Ba-da-ba-da-ba-da-ba-da-ba-da-ba-da.

And threw the bundle down:

Flummmmmmmmmm!

Then the Kano man ran back to the well and looked down. 'Got you at last,' he shouted down the well. 'You'll never get out of there, you cheap Katsina swindler.'

And the well replied, 'Swindler – swindler – indler – dler – dler.'

The Kano man picked up one of the stones by the well and dropped it down the hole:

Weeee-uuuu. Flummmm!

And another stone:

Weeee-uuuu. Flummmm!

Keep it up! But he took his time because he was thinking what he'd do with all the money he got from selling the loot.

MEANWHILE

back among the bundles behind the Kano man's back, that last, heavy bundle moved. It moved. And who do you think came out? Yes, none other than:

181

D-DNNNNN
THE KATSINA MAN

Well now, the Katsina man had to work very fast to get all those bundles moved to another place before the Kano man finished throwing the stones down the well. So the Katsina man will need your help, won't he . . . ? . . .

Right then, push your sleeves up! You know all about bundle-moving by now, don't you? So get on with it! And don't forget those stones:

Hey-up!
Pa-ta-pa-ta-pa-ta-pa-ta-pa-ta-pa-ta.
Flummm!
Pa-ta-pa-ta-pa-ta-pa-ta-pa-ta-pa-ta-pa-ta.
Hey-up!
Weeee-uuuu. Flummmm!

Slower on the stones there! Faster on the bundles! Faster, faster! Come on. Press your fast forward buttons! Keep it up!

Pa-ta-pa-ta-pa-ta

The big question now is: will the Katsina man finish before the Kano man? He's running very fast indeed, he's nearly finished. But so has the Kano man. Will he? Won't he? Will he? Yes, he will. He's done it, the Katsina man. Stop moving the bundles now. He's moved all the bundles and hidden himself behind a big boulder, quite out of breath. And there's the last stone down the well.

182

Weeee-uuuu. Flummmm

The Kano man's finished now and he's strolling over to where he left the bundles, rubbing his hands.

But now he's rubbing his eyes. He's looking and looking. He can't believe it. No loot! Not a bundle to be seen! He dashes round frantically for a few minutes looking behind every bush. Then he stops and laughs.

'Well, of course,' he says to himself. 'Of course! I would have done the same myself. That cunning Katsina chap! He was in that last bundle. That's why it was so heavy. Well, he can't have moved all those bundles far all by himself. He'll need some help. And I, the cleverest man in Kano, am going to be the one who provides him with help.'

So, the Kano man walked off a little way and hid behind a bush. There he began to bray like a donkey:

He-haw! He-haw! He-haw! He-haw!

MEANWHILE

back among the bundles the Katsina man was stretched out on the brocade, waiting for sunset. Suddenly he heard a donkey – dozens of donkeys, in fact. He jumped up. 'That's just what I need, you know,' he said. 'That's great! Sounds like a herd of donkeys. They can carry the loot for me.' And off he ran to find the donkeys:

'Tut-tut-tut-tut-tut!

Here boy! Carrot, carrot, carrot!' He didn't have any

carrots, of course. He swindled donkeys as well as people, you see!

'Here boy! Here boy! Carrot, carrot, carr . . . So, you're the donkey, are you? I might have guessed.'

And there they were again, toe to toe, face to face; the Kano man crocodiling down at the Katsina man:

eeeeeee!

And the Katsina man crocodiling up at the Kano man:

eeeeeee!

The Kano swindler spoke first, 'Clever trick that, down in the well, my good fellow. But not clever enough to fool me. Let's say no more about this unfortunate incident, shall we? Tell me, there's a good chap, where have you hidden the stuff?'

The Katsina man took him to the pile of merchandise and the Kano man said, 'I think it's high time we put a stop to all this childish trickery, don't you think, my good man?'

'You took the words right out of me mouth, like,' said the Katsina man. 'Stupid, us trying to cheat each other and that. We'll go halves. Gentleman's agreement?'

And they shook hands once more, toe to toe, face to face, crocodiling at each other:

eeeeeeeeeeeeeeee!

The Kano swindler said, 'My house is not so far from here. Let me invite you to stay with me. I'll tell my servants to carry all this stuff over there and then it will be in no danger, will it?'

'Er! No! I suppose not,' said the Katsina man.

So all the loot was carried to the Kano swindler's

house and stacked in the store room. The Katsina man stayed there overnight.

The next morning he said to the smooth-faced Kano man, 'I got to go home now, you know, and see how the old folks are. But I'll be back in three months with my servants to carry my half of the stuff away. Ta very much for the grub and bed and that. Don't run away with the loot. I'll make a swindler's agreement with you on that. Cheers then, mate.'

'A swindler's agreement it shall be,' said the Kano man. 'Goodbye, my dear fellow. Sorry to see you go. Take care.'

Nearly three months passed and the loot was still there. The Kano man made his servants dig a grave. He climbed down inside the grave and made them pile the earth back over him, leaving air holes so he could breathe.

And sure enough, later that day there was a knock at the door and who should it be but:

D-DNNNNN
THE KATSINA MAN

Everybody in the house started wailing. The women were wailing and tearing their hair out:
    Waaaa! Waaaa! Waaaa! Waaaa! Waaaa!
And the men were gnashing their teeth and raising their arms to heaven;
    Ergh! Ergh! Ergh! Ergh! Ergh! Ergh!
That's right. It sounds good!

In the middle of it all the Katsina man came in, 'What's going on here, then? Why all this screaming?' he asked.

'The master died two days ago.
Waaaa! Waaaa!
We buried him this morning,
Ergh! Ergh!'
'Oh aye,' said the Katsina man. He didn't believe a word of it, of course. He'd heard real wailing before, done by the merchants. And he noticed the women weren't really pulling their hair out.
'Oh aye! I'm very sorry to hear that, like,
Ergh! ergh!
He was a good friend of mine, you know. Can you show me to his grave? I want to pay my friend my last respects, like,
Ergh! ergh!'
When he got to the grave, he bowed his head and

said, 'Ah well, it comes to the best of us in the end, like,

Ergh! ergh!

May he rest in peace and that! But I see' (and he raised his voice a bit) 'you haven't got no protection for the grave. Put some thorn bushes over the grave to keep the hyenas off. They love eating bodies that have just died. They come in the night, you know, and start digging. I wouldn't want my friend's body to come to no harm, like,

Ergh! ergh!'

MEANWHILE

down in the grave the Kano swindler heard all this and he started sweating, buckets of water pouring off him.

Come on! Act sweaty! Use your imagination!

He hadn't thought of hyenas. He was really scared of being eaten.

Then they all went back into the house and the Katsina man said, 'Give us a bed for the night. I'll kip here and be on my way tomorrow, like.'

In the middle of the night the Katsina man got up and you know where he went, don't you?

No, not to the toilet, funny boy! He went to the grave. And there he began to scrabble at the earth and whimper and snuffle like a hungry hyena:

pfff! pfff! ew! ew! scrabble-scrabble! pfff! pfff!

Down in the grave the Kano man had had enough. He thought it was a real hyena coming to eat him. HELP! HELP! HELP! HELP!

'All right then, you can come out now, clever dick!' said the Katsina man. 'You didn't think I was going to fall for that cheap trick, did you?'

The Kano man crawled out. And there they were again, toe to toe, face to face, crocodiling at each other:

eeeeeeeeeeeeeeee!

. . . Are you getting tired of this story yet?"

"NO"

"No? Well, I've had enough. If you want any more, you can make it up yourselves. The rat's tail is off. That's the end."

And the next story was
THROWN OUT
Yes, Thrown out! Head over heels!
All together now!
Aaaaaah!
But it picked itself up and
waifed around till it found a hole in the
book binding. It crept inside and lay down
here at the back, hoping the editor wouldn't notice,
and longing for somebody to tell it,
somebody small and young, like you.
It's only a little one, and easy enough for you too to tell.
Once more, all together now!
Aaaaaah!
I haven't the heart to throw it out again. So, here it is.

Mouse

One evening not so long ago among the Ekoi people of
Nigeria, Agra of Mbeban, the marvellous teller of
tales, sat, waiting till the time was ripe. And while he
sat, night slowly spread its black hood across the
sunbright sky:

blacker blacker blacker BLACK

Through the blackness the very faintest of faint light
from a million million pinholes glimmered. With him
in the starlit darkness sat shadow children and shadow
parents, shadow me and shadow you, and quietly
talked and waited. Here and there, hardly noticed by
any of us, flitted shadow mice, each one with a tale to
tell. But Agra of Mbeban, the great word weaver,
heard the tales the mice squeaked. He chose one and
began:

"I hear that at night Mouse goes everywhere, search-
ing and collecting. With whiffly nose and twitching
whiskers she darts through the houses of the rich. She
visits even the poorest folk. Her bright eyes watch the
doing of secret things. She can tunnel into the sec-
retest treasure room and see what's hidden there.

189

There's no place safe from Mouse.

Long long ago on moonless nights Mouse began to make stories out of everything she'd seen. And for each story she wove a gown of a different colour – white, red, blue, yellow, purple, green and every shade between. She had no children of her own, so these stories became her children. They lived with her in her house, taking care of her and talking to her on starry nights till the black hood of night drew back and day dawned.

But one night in the street right outside Mouse House there was a fight. Her front door was old and it collapsed. All the tales escaped and flooded the world. And that's why there are always tales to tell today."

THE VERY END

Well, that was the end of the book, but it isn't the end for you. It's a beginning: the beginning of learning to tell a tale in your own way, as I've told these African tales in my way. Everybody's got tales to tell and everybody's got their own way of telling tales; and "everybody" means you too, doesn't it? And what's more, you've got everything you need to go and tell a tale.

You've read or heard these tales, haven't you?
You know other tales, don't you?
You have friends, haven't you?
You have a voice, haven't you?
You have a tongue, haven't you?
There you go . . .

THE MAN WITH A TREE ON HIS HEAD

Hus - band mine, what's
that__ strange thing I can see that's grown up - on your head?
(Repeat 3 times)

Lis - ten here, lis - ten here, tree man. Was - n't
(Chorus: Listen here, listen here, tree man.)

it a tree on your head, tree man? Was - n't

it me__ who made you well, tree man? Was - n't
Was - n't

it a pro - mise that you made, tree man?
it a cow that you pro - mised, tree man?

THE GOOD HERDBOY

Herd boy, will you tell on me, herd boy? Nev-er will I

tell. Hot soup, don't you eat it up, hot soup. Nev-er will I

tell. Cold milk, that's the thing for you, cold milk.
(Repeat: Never will I tell.)

SOURCES

1. Nyar-upoko: adapted from *Myths and Legends of the Congo*, Dr Jan Knappert; Heinemann, 1971.

2. Zazamankh: in most collections of ancient Egyptian writings.

3. The Man with a Tree on his Head: adapted from *Mainane: Tswana Tales*, ed. Shusheela Curtis; Botswana Book Centre, Gaborone, 1975.

4. The Bag of Money: adapted from *Folktales from the Gambia*, © Emile A. Magel; Three Continents Press, Washington DC, 1984.

5. The Good Herdboy: adapted from *African Oral Literature for Schools*, Jane Nandwa and Austin Bukenya; by permission of Longman, Kenya, 1983.

6. Karimirwa and Musiguku: my own source.

7. There's One Day for the Victim: adapted from *Not Even God is Ripe Enough*, Gbadamosi, B. and Beier, U.; Heinemann, 1968.

8. Hare and the White Man: my own source.

9. Hare and his Friends: adapted from *Keep My Words: Luo Oral Literature* , Onyango-Ogutu, B. and Roscoe, A.A.; East African Publishing House, 1974.

10. Dubulihasa: adapted from *The Xhosa Ntsomi*, Scheub, H.; © Oxford University Press, 1975.

11. *Omutugwa*: my own source.

12. The Wise Little Girl: adapted from *Reynard the Fox or Hottentot Fables and Tales*, Bleek, W.H.I.; Trubner & Co, 1864.

13. The Two Swindlers: adapted from *A Selection of African Prose, Vol. I*, translated by Court, J.W.; compiled by Whiteley, W.H.; Oxford University Press, 1964.

Mouse: adapted from *In the Shadow of the Bush*, Talbot, P.A.; Heinemann, 1912.